Gasping for Air

Stories of Adults and Children

by

Katherine Trace Brueck

Finishing Line Press
Georgetown, Kentucky

Gasping for Air

Stories of Adults and Children

This chapbook was made possible in part by donations to the ONE LAST WORD Program. ONE LAST WORD helps to bring the last works of gifted poets to the world.

Publisher: Leah Huete de Maines

Editor: Christen Kincaid

Cover Art: Photocase-photo storm 02 by 3bke.de
Licence-lD: 5791081 / Photo-ID: 65776 / July 1 6, 2022 / Size: L/ Basic Licence 6.0

Author Photo: Marcy Dugan

Cover Design: Elizabeth Maines McCleavy

Order online: www.finishinglinepress.com
             also available on amazon.com

Author inquiries and mail orders:
Finishing Line Press
PO Box 1626
Georgetown, Kentucky 40324
USA

Contents

PERSONAL STORIES OF ADULTS AND CHILDREN

CONTEMPORARY STORIES OF ADULTS AND CHILDREN

CLASSIC STORIES OF ADULTS AND CHILDREN

To our daughters Emily and Heidi

Personal Stories of Adults and Children

Witch in a Wig

Mama, this morning, why did you breathe like a dragon when I would not put on my rain boots? Your tresses were flying like a witch's hair as you took my umbrella and beat the carpet dry until the rains came.

This afternoon, when you saw me walk in the front door for lunch, you turned away. You climbed into the attic, wearing holes for eyes.

This evening when you looked at me after school, before Daddy came home, why did you begin to undress? Why did you go out of the house, why did you walk toward the bus stop wearing only your slip and the red hat you and I bought together last Wednesday?

My gentle, my childlike mama: I know, at such times, someone buries you deep, deep beneath the soil in a grave, beneath a tomb with no name.

Papa, please. Daddy, protect me. Build a playhouse for me. Anywhere where I can hide when Mama leaves the real world, when she goes where witches in wigs and madwomen go.

Please, Daddy, please.

Babyland

Neither of them wanted me to live. So you see I don't live. Not really. Here in Babyland—no, I'm not a Babe in Toyland—I'm in Babyland. Where the cold wind blows.

Those two—my almost-mother and my almost-father: they didn't want me to come into the world. So, I didn't.

I came to Babyland instead, where I am and, I sense, I will always be an almost-baby.

An almost-baby, though, with thoughts and, somehow, language though not speech. Someone's strange gifts to a near-baby. A baby like me.

I heard them talking from inside. Inside the womb. "I need to get rid of her," she used to say.

"Yes…of course," he said in a curt but strangely gentle voice, and then added, "I will pay."

They thought they'd get rid of me. But they didn't. I was here listening to them. To both of them whenever they mentioned me. Now if their current partners hint anything about my near-existence, I can hear them speaking nervously.

Always they are nervous when they speak of me.

I understand why: talking about someone who never made it into their world but threatened to.

Every once in a while, I knock on the side of the ice block where I dwell: *Tap tap tap.*

No one hears me, though.

I am frozen here, frozen forever.

They decided.

They are warm. Warm with life.

What does that mean?

That is something I will never know, I guess.

I, in my ice block. Frozen here like a baby gone bad.

Or, I guess, just gone.

Betrayal

Judas…a flaming torch…Judas.

He enters the garden, the garden of evening. The girl awakes from sleep. She walks toward Judas, the father in the house. Judas comes forward, he walks slowly, always forward: is that love on his face?

a reaching out

two and two…he breaks them

he breaks two breasts with two hands

one and ten

he breaks one heart with ten fingers

sullies, shatters

a living soul

her soul?

The father in the house

Judas

flaming torch

Judas

Said, "Now is the daughter of woman glorified."

Black-Horned Toad

Fire and ice,

a frenzy of feeling let loose: live doll in scarlet silently calling "Mommy, Mommy,"

as she comes crying then laughing into the arms of my heart, into the being of my soul,

into the apple core of my raspberry caress.

Now only a black-horned toad can rob me of my treasure: in day or in night.

Blake

Mama, he broke his hands. Five years ago, he broke them. It was the boy who went to jail—yeah, that's the one—the drug addict. He broke his hands. He broke them for me.

Remember? I was in middle school. I went with Ava to the Coldplay concert. Blake, he couldn't stand it. He wanted me to stay with him. But we had tickets—Ava and I. We went and rocked, we tossed the stars till dawn.

His fingers one by one broke in two while my friend and I leapt across the abyss till the sun bowed down and died.

I held his hands in jail—I remember I left my schoolwork and sat with him in the jail and held his hands. I sat with him till the sun bowed down. Till it bowed down and died.

Or did I sit with him until nightfall but only in a dream?

Blake is out of jail now. He roams the bars. A night prowler. Untamed.

He's so nervous, he can't sit still. He has a tattoo. He got it in jail. A tattoo that covers his whole body. A tattoo called shame that is his only souvenir from Jail Land. Yes, I've seen it.

His mom ran a recovery house. For addicts. Why didn't they let him go there? Remember? I wonder. Next time, if the Animal People catch Blake before the cops do, maybe he'll be lucky and he'll sit behind bars in the shelter, with the other animals, waiting for the herculean arms of a man to embrace him or for the soft breast of a woman to give him suck.

You're quiet, Mama. Just like you were quiet when Blake fucked me. Remember, when he came to our house and fucked me? Remember that?

I wanted him to. I wanted him to fuck me. Because he had broken his hands. He had broken them for me. For no one else but me.

It was the least I could do. I let him enter me at will on that day.

Did you ever read his poetry? He respects you, you know. He took an interest in you because you took an interest in him. I used to give your hellos to him, I filled his empty pants and shirt pockets with your hellos when I left my college books to visit him in jail.

Maybe you were like a kind, curious guard who watches as a prisoner plays out his days howling in blood and ebony.

That's right. There was the suicide attempt. Two years before his first arrest. He sent me pictures of the gashes he'd cut into his wrists and arms. He sent them to me on my phone. He tried to kill himself because I had found another boyfriend that year.

I had to, Mama, or I could not have lived or loved any longer. You understand that, don't you?

Remember the dog we saw in Turkey? The one with only three legs? You liked it, remember? That dog was just like you, Mama. He was missing a leg, just like you.

Blake is like that.

Maybe that's why I'm still friends with Blake. In spite of everything.

Because he is like that dog, and he is also like you.

Yes. Blake is like my mama, my own mama.

No. He's not respectable. He's not a member of the comfortable class.

Still. Like you he dwells in a black reservoir.

I think you know that. That's why you've always taken an interest.

Yes.

We three: we're the crucified ones.

We live on a wild, a scorched earth, a barren field where anything goes.

We gasp for air in a black reservoir haunted by the cry of God.

Blood and Nails

Wrinkles over blue denim descended stairs of oak. Two ripe full breasts walked forward with sadness and grace beneath dark eyes and hair.

She carried an infant, sleeping now, smiling with serenity born of newness and age.

I touched her, my daughter, I covered my breast and locked into aged eyes and said, "Bear me. Bear me away to Palestine where spirits linger. Take me where Jesus died, where he lived, bore children, including you and me, then died on a cross for love."

"I cannot," my daughter said.

"Mama, you dream and live in dreams. I must return now to Joe: I will wash his dirty clothes and then his hair, I will pay his bills and scrub the kitchen floor. I will take out board games and spread them throughout the hall for the amusement of my children and his.

"I will not go to Palestine. I will stay with my man and our boys. This little one can go with you, though. Take her and find new life."

She gave me the infant, turned, and climbed stairs of oak, then disappeared into her life of duty, to boys and man. A man confined to a life of paralysis in a chair.

I smiled at the little one.

I had no milk to give.

Still, I took out one of my breasts and she sucked the round nipple as we walked across the water to Palestine, where we saw no grim trace of the daily: only mystery of blood and nails and sacrifice. The babe and I were lifted up for the life of the world.

We died there for a world we loved. We died for my daughter and for Joe and their boys. We suffered and died for the daily misery of the cold and warm hearts of the barren earth we had left behind.

Bride in Bloom

The day I bought my wedding dress was the day I learned about my mama.

I learned something I had not known before. Had I looked I would have seen.

Rodeo Drive, Beverly Hills: that was where I performed for her. As I had never performed before.

While I tried on bridal gowns, I was happy as a duckling swimming before the moon.

Gold held my reflection: a bride in bloom.

The dress I chose rose and walked with me; a halo of gems illumed my way.

In celebration, Mama and I shared a meal on green grass.

On our way home she did not respond to me in her usual way.

Frightened, I yelled at her.

Mama was mostly silent.

We reached her home, and I walked in with her, still not understanding.

"I didn't sleep well last night…I…"

She looked at me through eyes I had not seen, had not noticed before.

Pleading eyes.

Eyes tired with time.

It was then I realized: my mama would be gone.

I might own the wedding dress.

I might even be married.

And to the same man.

But my mother would be no more.

Bird of death: arrow floating in the rain.

Daddy's Women

Sensuality was a cross for you, Daddy. And for me.

In days of adolescence and adulthood—

Fire in your eyes burned me until mute ash piled up where my voice used to be, a tortured voice writhing in flames.

Her bare breasts burned my loins and also yours. We were partners, twins, in the red pool of iniquity.

You, the black man, I, the child white with innocence and embers.

Breast and skin: "Only one breast, please, with skin…No, two of them: two breasts with skin, please."

As I heard you order, I felt a dying inside. A falling away. Followed by the waves that drown.

Dirty pictures

would appear

on paper and on film.

What would Father say?

The good one who left us nailed to the cross:

the cross of the naked man-god who lived and died in the sky.

Darkness and Stars

When I was a very small child I frolicked in the land of liberty. I blithely let my mother choose riotous, pink-striped frames for my eyeglasses, and, depending on the weather, I wore either a French beret or an Eskimo hat when I went shopping with mother.

I did not enter the dark cell until my eighth summer when we took our first family vacation. My mother and sister were almost asleep in the motel room when my father, my daddy whom I loved, looked at me. He looked at me like a snake looks when he slithers upward and stares into your eyes. "Thin!" he said. "Your hair is so thin, you look like a freak. Your ears stick up right through it."

For the first time in my short life, I walked into the dank, dark cell. The cell of shame.

When I was twelve, the daddy whom I still loved pointed to Connie of the beautiful curls, to Susan of the dark eyelashes, to Mary of the round bosoms, and smiled.

Then he looked at my picture in the school album.

"You are," he said, "a rock in your own rock pile."

A rock belongs in prison—I knew that. A rock does not need to grow or to reach toward the stars. A rock is not a flower.

Over the next three years my older sister became the rose of an hour. She flirted with a blue-eyed boy in the kitchen of our summer inn in Ireland. Jealousy made me cringe.

On Fridays there was a dance at the inn. To that first dance I wore a pretty crinkled top over a flat chest and a striped skirt.

A boy approached and asked me to be his partner.

I said yes and smiled.

"Iron?" he said. "You wear those iron things," he said with a brogue and a laugh.

My braced teeth did not belong in public. Although I had let them out that evening. It was I who had let them out.

That night I felt the darkness, the dampness of the prison I somehow knew I was not to be released from. My confinement was solitary. Parole would never come. This I knew.

Despair whispered in my ear,

"A train.

"Take an express train to heaven."

By your holy cross you have redeemed the world.

By some miracle, during the next twenty-five years my appearance began to charm. These years as a flower, while I enjoyed them, were fragile, always moving toward extinction, an extinction I had already tasted, I had already been privileged to taste, as a young girl.

Five years ago, I became an amputee.

My amputation reminds me of my early years in prison. Those childhood years I embrace now as I do nothing else.

During my years as a young girl, during my years as convict, I had begun to taste the truth, an absolute truth, a truth I was never to know clearly or fully until now, when I come closer and closer once again to the great mystery at the heart of things: the love that fashions the darkness and the stars.

Dona Nobis Pacem

Little brown-haired Louisa rolled an enormous stone down the center aisle of the church.

Her seven-year-old fingers blistered as she pushed the behemoth forward. The rock kept rolling back. But she ran with it. She ran forward toward the sacristy. She bounced and bounced back in the dimness of church day.

Four hours later she heard someone say, "Open the door. Come in."

The little girl took her heavy burden and squished it into the dark box: the train stop from which the tired voice had traveled.

The rock cramped, crushed against the wall of the confessional. She whispered, "Bless me father for I have sinned. This is my first confession."

The boulder exploded, all lights extinguished: the innocent one lay dead, dead to ease and joy.

The priest lived on. Alive and in control. He muttered to himself:

Miserere nobis.

Miserere nobis.

Have mercy on us.

Dona nobis pacem.

Give us peace.

Dona nobis pacem.

The old man's chanting could be heard within and outside the beautiful edifice of stone and shame.

Finger Painting

Into the night.

Like a bird with one wing.

Peace I called it.

Freedom beneath the moon.

Where is she flying now?

Is she moaning low?

Shrieking for quietness?

"I have to go up North. Yes, yes, I'll change my number. He won't be able to send more pictures. More threats, more finger paintings of his cherished, his cherry suicide, his black exit in the rain.

"His footprints, his fingerprints—I could not escape them here.

"My bird, my bird with one wing. Go, fly," I said. "Go, fly…"

I didn't find a box for her—and settle her in it.

Nor did I choose a medic who could fix her wing.

Instead, I gave her what she asked me for—the black night and the freedom to enter and dwell in that night all summer long.

"I forbid you nothing," I said.

When she vanished, she pointed the poker of her absence at my heart and burned it raw.

Why did she not speak her games of freedom, her riotous clubs, her soarings in the air with one wing?

When she emerged from the darkness, she was gasping for air.

Her air.

Yes, she returned…with tales of Redwood Trees, a drunken smile and a pocketful of cannabis.

She had—I could tell—a new sense that all the world was a stage.

Her stage.

"I lost him, the thought of him, and his suicide threats haunt no more," she said, bleary-eyed, reaching for the fridge in her room.

She drank one beer and then another, collapsing her wing beneath her.

She lay sprawled on her bed with a smile of longing and pain.

Her longing, it was her longing and her pain. Coming south she brought those souvenirs for her mama. They satisfied.

"I am satisfied," I said, as I stared into a lake ringed by willows, a lake that flows by the moon.

"Have I found it, Mama? Have I found the quietness you spoke of: freedom beneath the moon?"

And she passed out, one wing folded neatly beneath her.

She passed out in a stupor of longing and pain.

Freeland

When I say something, no one looks at me. When I draw a question mark in the air, no one hears. On Wednesdays I put a pacifier in my mouth—no one cares.

In class this morning I needed to go to the bathroom before recess. Before I could raise my hand—a pool of pee was flowing. Flowing on the floor. Why? Why did it flow without me? And why did my classmates stare at me? Why did they stare like wolves?

I am a loner, I admit it. At times, though, I have thought someone liked me. For weeks in the morning, at 9:00, Father Mark came to talk to the fifth graders. He looked at me—I know he did—I remember because I smiled at him, as I often did. I took the pacifier out of my mouth just for Father Mark so we could smile at one another. He returned my smile! But in the past several weeks Father has looked at Brenda, not at me. I don't blame him. Everyone looks at Brenda—especially when like today her mother let her hazel hair flow down over her shoulders and over her shapely breasts and down even to her knees.

They made me come back to class after recess—after my 11:00 pee. I decided then that I wasn't going to come back to school anymore. Not after today. No, I decided, school isn't for me—my older sister Annie likes it...or she used to before she went on a motorcycle ride with my neighbor and died with him. But I decided I am never going to go back to school, not after they tortured me with my own piss.

Instead, I am going to find a place where I won't need a pacifier or a toilet or a mirror to store my flaws in. I am going to find a grassy meadow where I will run with horses in a forest and where I will burn all night from the stars dying in my eyes, and where red flames will light up my dead heart.

Please don't come with me or I will never be able to find a land I can call my own.

Hilda

Hilda, I will always remember Hilda.

Dark-skinned, swelling breasts, one long black braid, she walked into our house that afternoon. Right through the door. No knock. She just walked in. She had never done that before.

She saw me that afternoon as no one else has—no one but medical staff and family. No one else in the world has seen me so nude, so humiliated, so me. But Hilda. Buck-toothed, sassy eighth grader, Hilda saw.

My stump was bare and hanging. No one in the neighborhood or at work or at the shopping mall had seen. My prosthesis makes me look normal, even if I don't walk quite right in it. Still, I look like a human being. I look whole when I wear a prosthesis on my right leg under a long skirt. Without it, I am a strange-looking animal. A freak. I only felt my own freakishness once, though. Once, since the doctor told me my right leg had been severed just below the knee. I had just woken up groggy from a minor operation gone wrong and he told me, "It was life or limb." While under deep morphine I had experienced what they call a "never event." At the hospital I experienced an event that should never have happened. I have since learned that thousands of them happen every day.

Only once since then have I felt to the marrow of my bones that I was a sideshow freak: the day young Hilda walked in and saw.

The door was unlocked but not open—she came in without knocking; she was looking for her pet beagle, Arnie. "I'm sorry!" she cried in a panic after she had had a good stare. She ran as fast as she could back through the door. Like a naked child faced by a man with a gun: I shrieked my shame.

Hilda used to babysit our cats when we went on vacation. Sometimes she even watched our granddaughter when we went to the movies or to dinner with our daughter and her boyfriend.

No more babysitting money for Hilda. No more rides to school or friendly visits. Hilda, the intruder, would be welcome in our home no more.

At the memory, still I shake like a naked child confronted by a man with a gun.

Now we'll have to move, my husband and I, we will have to move to a safe place, one like our home was for many years, a place where no one will know I am an amputee in peacetime: a fucking freak.

Dark-skinned mysterious Hilda will not pay except in small ways.

But my psyche has been branded.

Burned by the horror, the humiliation.

My very soul has been bruised with the arms and legs the hospital casually severs and tosses—some the garbage of war, others, like mine, carved in silence during peace.

Yes, I will always remember Hilda:

Young, carefree, whole.

Hilda is the stuff of dreams.

Joe and I

It was past midnight, or seemed to be, when we arrived at the graveyard: you and I.

"We can hide here tonight…until he comes. He will come," I whispered to you, sleeping infant, who cannot hear.

Your daddy, Joe, had looked so gentle this morning, his hair tousled in the daylight, shining like a Japanese lantern in our bleak and cold, our somber living space.

Joe who no longer is. Joe who will take his place here soon. I look at the tombstones by the white round star. Here where they put us in the soil so we can sleep again. As soundly as when we were babies, babies in the womb or at the breast.

As soundly as you, Jude, Jude my darling. Joe had called you "breast-sucker" every morning for three days. Joe's constant drunken taunts: "Jude the hopeless cause," "Jude the leech," "Jude the tiny son of a bitch."

Your daddy was loving at first, but he became mean a few months after you, my treasure, my lovely one, were born. Your dad began to say I had abandoned him. I left him for the baby who was sucking me, when I should have been sucking him. That's what he said.

"Jude the curse that came in the darkness." He had a whole list of hate words for you, my innocent one. You, it is true, had come unlooked-for one morning in a month without name.

My lover of five years, the beautiful Joe, looked so gentle as he sat in the kitchen this morning. He wasn't gentle, though. He was drunk. Drunk from a binge the night before, the binge that carried on into morning. He was still blind drunk. I saw his anger against you, building until he opened the kitchen drawer and took out a knife. But I blocked the black path of certainty. Seized by a terrible bad-fear, I did what I knew I had to do. I knew it would have been only a matter of time and you, my baby, would be in mortal danger. Threatened by your own father. You my baby, I feared, would be killed if I did not act.

Then we came here, you and I. Here is where the policeman will come. I await the gravedigger who pulled me from the womb, as he once did Joe. The gravedigger came for your daddy this morning and soon he will come for me. Is that an officer's cap? Is it over for you and for me, little Jude? I whispered all this to the blessed being who slept without knowing.

Now, only now, I see them: I see them in the earth…deep under the graves: the bones of God. Bones gnawed raw by love of the world.

Julia

There she is again: curly blonde hair, white skin, large black eyes.

Five times now she has come to me in the night. She never speaks. She might be of speaking age. I don't know. She never cries. She just looks at me: her eyes hollow with bewilderment.

Jeff is sometimes with me when she comes. Sometimes not.

I love Jeff. When we make love, at that special moment, he says to me, "I love you." Do I hallucinate when he says at climax, "I love you"?

Do I?

Jeff comes and goes, like the pretty girl-child.

I lied, you know. I lied when I said she never speaks. She does say one word—I never know when she's going to say it. "Mommy." Where did she learn to say that word?

Her hair is cute and curly, as if having been set in spoolies, like my mom said hers was set when she was a child. Julia's hair curls naturally like mine. She doesn't need spoolies. It's bushy, too. Bushy like my own. Not Mom-thin. Her skin is white like feathers or the snow. Her black eyes glow like coals flickering as a fire dies.

Jeff is with me again tonight. As before, I tell him about the child. I feel I speak to a wall when I tell him, a wall without a chink, a prison wall.

He watches movies on TV. Or plays games on my screen. When he walks around the room, he doesn't know what he does. I am sure he doesn't: he walks right through her.

When we make love, he says at climax, "I love you." I know he cherishes me, body and soul.

"We made her, you know," I say.

Now she is gone again. This time she disappeared as Jeff left for work. I would kill her if I could. But I can't. She is a phantom, a phantom who comes between me and my boyfriend. She looks innocent, but she is mean. She is mean because she comes between me and my love.

She is not like the rat that came every night for two weeks. The rat was real. It was real and ugly. Jeff and I finally trapped it. We trapped it together. And then it was gone. Together we threw the smelly carcass into the garbage. We smiled in unison as we cast it away.

Julia is unreal and beautiful. I cannot trap her. I actually tried it once. On my own. I made a child-trap—put a bowl of milk out for bait. She acted like it wasn't there. She just stared at me with her hollow black eyes, her body white like the snow and her bushy blonde hair that curls naturally like mine.

She ignored the bait. She just looked at me wide-eyed. She looked for a whole minute. Then she said it; she said it two times:

"Mommy."

"Mommy."

Let you go?

Your spirit roams though you have gone.

Your single visit curses my newborn child.

You set a fire on the balcony without remembering.

Years ago, you destroyed our home: you drove through the front window. Without remembering.

Fleeing to the East, could you find a different you?

Or did you find a hospital with a special ward: Pathos.

I struggle every day not to become another you.

Will wife and child wrap me in their arms? Will they tow me to the beautiful isle: Sobriety?

Mom won't sign the papers: your gateway to freedom.

She hates you: your infidelities and unseemliness.

Is that why she won't let you go?

Or is it what you have done to her children?

Is it the legacy you leave behind you that terrifies?

That inspires a hatred so pure that she cannot let you go?

Magic or Gold

You won't grow. You won't run and hide in the bushes with me.

You plant yourself, baby-child, in the moment's soil.

You won't speak in words or even letters. Your head bobs in silence until a scream wiggles ghostlike from your infantine cave.

You wake from wailing wide-eyed and dance to the lily music: the feel of home, the lingering touch of the womb.

You won't rise and walk to the bushes and hide with me there. You lie on your back cooing with a cooer's tongue, gurgling, smiling a prehuman smile.

But why won't you grow as I look on? Why, my grandbaby?

Speak the mystery, the mystery in the shroud of life's heart. Why won't you grow as I look on, beady-eyed?

Why won't you rise and lead me to the bushes and huddle with me there?

Your gift of nonsense in the day, your present of stillness in the night—in them dwells not one word: only magic or gold.

Mail

We live here and we don't live here. People must know. The mail carrier must know this address isn't where we live. Although I suppose you could say we reside here.

The pink tea tree, the grass brown from drought, the Siamese cat next door with its one-bell collar are all there for us. But they are not there, too.

Maybe we should abandon the house. We could even burn it. Or we could move in permanently—bring furniture here and red flowers and a dog. And him, of course—Joseph. We could bring him.

Maybe sometime the mail will stop coming altogether. Or maybe the right mail will come. That would be nice. If we got letters or even bills addressed to us. Bills we could pay. It would be nice to have a home.

I hear someone crying. Sounds like hunger or fear. Or maybe terror. Terror like I felt last night when I dreamed I was being pushed off an ocean liner and was falling toward the water. There were brown logs in the water. When I saw them, I knew I was falling to certain death.

It must be Joseph. I hear him cry like that sometimes. Usually in the evening. That's when we talk about him. His cry sounds like horror, horror that says, "I have no home but the womb. No home but the womb." There, though, it has stopped. If only his terror would kill him. Abortion wasn't made for us, or adoption, either. We are a unit, Bill: you and Joseph and I. But if terror would kill the baby, you and I could be free. We could go out and see the redwood trees in Northern California like we have dreamed, or Morro Bay on the sea.

But Joseph's terror is not life-threatening. I know it's not. And it will never be. Not as long as he is inside me. Instead, we will take a day at a time. We will wait and see. Maybe someday the mail will actually come. Someday we will have a house, and mail of our own will come to us from somewhere outside the womb. For now, this is where we live, all three of us—you and Joseph and me—in a womb away from the world: no address—no past—no future.

For now, though, there is no water. Only the water that drowns.

Mommy.

26

Fire and ice, a frenzy of feeling let loose: live doll in scarlet, silently calling.

He came crying, then laughing into the arms of my heart, into the beating of my soul, into the apple core of caress.

Only the black-horned toad can rip my son from me.

Only a toad black as night.

Mother-World

They pronounced her mine.

"Yours," they said. "She is yours."

"Pin her to you. Let her feed."

Blood runs down my breast into my womb. The womb that nourished her, then spewed her out like a cannonball in war.

She feeds like an enemy leech.

When will I find the lost one? The self. My self.

The baby drinks: with every gulp of milk comes the taste of blood. The blood of life. My life.

My boyfriend will get well. I know he will.

If he does not, I will pine alone in the canyon of desire: the desire to rise and walk again.

I bury myself deeper into the cave of sorrow with each breast the serpent carves.

My baby tempts and betrays with every hour of confinement, with every moment of mouth-gagging, with every day of sunlight hidden by a darkness that will not end.

Like a stranger, a heedless visitor of ill intent, she has positioned herself in my crib, the crib of desolation.

No.

My baby, my serpent, will not fade with the morning dew.

And nor will I, a twisted heart who longs for white barrenness in the black sea of fertility.

In the glass house of happiness, I bare my breast again, my wounded nipple, to the stone gaze of mother-world.

Out of the Debris

I fall into the vortex, whooshing away from my place in the world, whooshing toward red-A annihilation from the community, from the sisterhood of touch and smile and welcoming eye.

When I was a child, mama birds nestled me but I was alone, tripping in a world full of yew trees. Now a blunder, a failure, a difference sends me again into the desolate forest, into the arms of a human heart that takes me in and casts me out, a beater that throws me away like an old, bloody, stinking pad, a pad of the month that covered my loins like an arm when I turned fourteen.

Now a Child comes out of the debris.

After the hour of my humiliation. Tunneling through. She comes. And she will not leave me. A babe comes out of the debris. My babe. Child of comfort. Child of the ages.

A soft, a nestling newborn:

She comes to stay.

Apple Tree.

Before sex came, we loved one another.

We were pals, Papa.

You took me into your bosom: I rested close.

I rested like a lamb bleating her fondness.

You touched me with joy:

joy of snowfall,

joy of summer sea.

You sprinkled my world with radiant glory: the glory of your heart.

One day I could not touch you with quietness.

Men and women in and out of pretty costumes knocked out our light.

The days of the untouched apple tree disappeared,

Never to return.

Poultice of Paternity

He took my lead pencil, and he drew a picture. He designed a human figure, then a load of logs, a winter landscape, and a cabin. The colored pencils in my box were flashing without me a beautiful sunny scene in red and brown, magnificent orange and blue. And white snow under and over all.

He handed the finished picture to me: "This will get you an A!" he said with a quick smile. "A for Angel, sweetie!" And he hugged me.

I felt my eyes losing their color, my heart stumbling in the cellar, my spirit being smothered beneath power.

For many years after that fourth-grade picture, I lived in beautiful snow country: deep white drifts of security, blizzards of cozy isolation, ice ponds of dependence.

My face did not glow with the frozen fire that raged within me until my father's death early this morning. Yes, his death emerged. And fire melted the ice. Now flames rage fast and furious, flames of orange and lemon gloriously destroy me. They put me in a delirium called danger. My danger. For life, for the rest of my, yes, life. No one else's. Mine.

I have shaken off the poultice of paternity. Now I consciously and freely expose my wounds to the world. For the first time I am no one's little girl. No more protection or condescension or robbery.

I will now have a cross of my own to climb and I can fully expose myself, on my own, to the world in all its barrenness and brutality.

If I expose myself on the cross with love, and only then will I behold the beauty of the world.

Runaway

Water carries me. It carries me downstream. I love the way it undulates, the way it washes me away.

Land is hard. Land and burning wood and leather on my hands. Land is hard when there is no wood to burn, no leather to warm me.

The cutting sword of certainty stripped me of land and wood and leather. After

he abandoned me, I looked and looked for somewhere safe to be. I reached and reached, baby in my arms—his baby—but nothingness filled the air. The air was empty.

My bottle—a corked bottle—was always full. She helped me to fill it. She helped me until she knew.

And then the baby came. Now my mother is out of reach. My mother and also my lover.

But water carries me. It carries us. The little one, clinging to my heart, is destitute. Destitute like me.

If he hadn't left us. If he had been true. True as the sun that rises in the spring or the snow that falls.

In winter, I could have touched the land, I could have loved the land. I could have lived on land.

Lived with him. We could have done that.

One morning he was gone. He with his emerald eyes, his eyes like jewels, and his hand like a womb for me. He was gone.

No more the fires on the beach in the glow of crackling stars. No more the feel of leather on my warm and happy hands. No more…

Sister Mary Agnes

"What do you think?"

Cathy of the beautiful bosoms sighed, looked at the watch and the book. She yawned a silence that startled like a bell.

But Sister's question seized me. It shook me out of my usual quietness.

"I!"

I could begin, I thought. At least begin. I could say I! I had never said the word before. Not in high school. Not in this institution where answers were provided and arranged in advance like pieces of meat and cheese.

I, clamped shut like an oyster, I grew a pearl in pain.

"Where do we get these desires?" I said.

"Where does the desire for meaning come from?" I said to the sister in uniform, the sister in front of me wearing the white and black uniform of Christian faith.

The Metamorphosis by Franz Kafka. That was the text. Meaning the subject.

"Very good." she said.

What was "very good?" Was desire the answer to the black witch, the key to veiling the face of horror and absurdity in the world?

The chick of uncertainty—tawdry yellow—emerged from a hard white shell. Since that day fifty years have drizzled, stoned, pelted weak days and nights into dark corners, sovereign shadows. For half a century circles of query, arrows of asking, have pierced my life at its core.

Class was over. Cathy of the beautiful bosoms, my idol, after casting a smile my way, flew majestically into a life without queries or puzzles, without corners or shadows that explode my world, the same world that she, treasure of existence, graces like a dove.

Teresa

Teresa lay picking her scab in the night.

The crust covered the whole of her forehead.

"Mommy, I can!

"I know I can!"

These words had streaked across the morning sky one week before as Teresa scooted to the right. The back seat of the 1955 Buick gave way. The faux leather made way before her.

"Teresa, you are too little!"

"Mommy, I can! I know I can!"

She had lifted the door handle. She was only four, she knew, but she would do it.

Her six-year-old sister had done it. Why couldn't she?

She was as good as her sister!

It was then, as she lifted the handle, that she tumbled out. She rolled down the mountain. She scrambled in blackness.

She felt something smash.

Her forehead shot against the curb.

A parade of blood marched down her forehead to her eyes, her lips and chin.

"Me-h-h-h…Me-h-h-h," she bleated.

"Me-h-h-h" was all she could say. She knew no other language.

The word of the weak comes from the place of prey, the cave of captivity.

Teresa remembered that day, the day her grandparents had come to visit. She wanted to show them that she was no longer a sheep, but a real human being.

Worthy of notice. She would do it: she would open the car door by herself and climb out.

This way she could say, "I am a human being."

"I matter."

"I matter just like you!"

As she fell asleep, dully picking her scab, she felt chained as she recited her one-word line, the only word she could utter,

"Me-h-h-h,

"Me-h-h-h,

"Me-h-h-h."

The Blood and the Father

In the afternoon she had had to shove the father of her baby out the door, she had had to push her own lover whom she still loved into the cold. Only the shadow, the torturous memory, of her beloved remained. The gentle boy could only work and drink. She had vowed abstinence when she left rehab two weeks before. She was addicted—as he was—and she knew it. But, unlike him, she wanted to recover her life: a lost life.

Eve had never been close to her mother, but her death two days after her return had singed her bones. Her mother had died of leukemia a few days before Eve discovered she herself was pregnant with her boyfriend's baby. A siren, a woman in Thailand, had lured her father to a foreign land. Eve had worshipped her father. He had been her only deity. But he was left vulnerable when his dying wife abandoned him. He might never return. His departure ran cruelly through Eve's veins.

"You see where your boyfriends get you!" "Loser," she had called each of my men in succession. Eve remembered the moment her sister, Esmerelda, eyes flashing an angry green, disappeared into the night. Her fashionable sister couldn't tolerate having a "lowlife," as she called her, a recovering alcoholic, for a sister—especially one who was pregnant and, to her complete disgust, was determined to keep the child.

Now sleep, not liquor, was Eve's only medication. She was exhausted that afternoon, the noontide when she had forced her lover into light. She was chained, chained now, chained deep into a lair of love and loss. She needed the peace of a lamb, living or dead. A peace she saw no signs of in her own dreary land, the land of barren earth.

The figure of a man being tortured loomed out of a daze in darkness. A young man who had been stripped to his underwear, his head pierced with nails— arms and legs hammered…he was uttering something through a moan. He cried out that his father had abandoned him.

There was blood. Blood on his hands…"the blood and the father"…He looked at her. He said, "The blood of the world…kiss the blood of the world on my hands…" He smiled, love in his eyes. Suddenly…a shriek of despair and terror. As the young man's head nodded, his lips, full red lips, seemed to move…as though gently creating silence, the silence of the lambs of the world.

The Cupboard

You said, Mama, you dreamed of your alcoholic father in a crowd, a simple crowd, a crowd of people. You were five. He was twenty-five. You told me that.

In your dream he held your hand. He held it tight. You felt safe and warm, you felt at home in the world. Your hand in the womb of the man who bore you. Who gave you life.

You told me nothing could harm you; nothing could strip you of the certainty of love in the world. You glimpsed this truth for the few moments before he let go. Then your fingers wandered, running terrified toward the Western Sea. They separated, the five fingers on your hand, until they no longer formed a hand. They were separate digits, each wandering alone in an alien, a barren space.

You told me this, Mama, the day Mark left me, the day Mark, who had vowed he would abide with me, the day he departed. You told me your dream on the day he disappeared from my life. The cupboard of life. The cupboard where bread used to be, the food of joy.

You told me the story of your dream so Marsha could hear, seven-year-old Marsha who had cried every night since her daddy left us, since the moment we saw: his clothes were gone, his jacket, his hands. The hands that used to stroke her hair by the light of evening stars.

Since then, the child's fingers began to wander toward the sunset where you fled years ago in a dream. You wanted us both to know there is a love, a living love, that dwells behind the door. Happiness smiles behind the entrance, living happiness. That is what haunts us, teases us: the treasure behind the door.

This is what you told your daughter and your granddaughter as they suffered on the wild green hill of desolation. As they wept purple tears on the hands and on the jacket that he failed to leave behind. He failed to leave behind his jacket or his hands for Marsha—or for me.

The River

It was summer.

The day camp was located in the same building where I had gone to kindergarten the year before.

We made vases, bookshelves, straw baskets.

I don't remember much else, except Miss Martin. Miss Martin taught woodshop at camp. She had been my teacher the previous year. Her voice rang like a bell when she said, as she did in the morning, "Your Father loves you, children. Never forget. He loves the little children who come unto him, just as Jesus did." Then she would smile. Her smile was natural, sweet, beautiful. Her smile walked over to me, every morning, caressed me, and whispered into my ear, "Peace."

I really have no memories of the camp days beyond those.

Except for one.

One memory I have never revealed: the black river.

In the forest behind the camp, I learned about the river.

The eternal slideshow came to me one hot day in July.

It was time for lunch.

After we ate, a group of us went into the woods on the edge of camp property.

We delved into the haunted and haunting group of trees in stark outline against the sky.

A yellow ball of light, naked, hovered above as we tumbled into the green of leaves.

Two boys and one girl wanted to show off in that minute, the moment of the afternoon sun.

The girl.

She took off her dress and T-shirt.

She said, laughing—

"Hit me!"

"Strike me now!"

It was Gail. She was new to the camp. She lived on my street.

Gail was pretty—she had a gap tooth. Physical charm had claimed her with a rare fierceness.

"Hit me!" she repeated, laughing.

She stuck out her bottom.

One of the boys pulled down her underpants and the other one broke a stick off a nearby bush.

They obeyed her command.

One at a time they struck her smooth round bottom: pale but glimmering.

She laughed. She laughed as though they were tickling her.

They beat her again in fun, in play.

She continued to laugh hilariously.

The rest of us were uneasy.

Gail's little brother, Eric, began to cry.

"We've got to get back," I said, trembling with an emotion that was new to me.

"Lunchtime is over," my friend Damien yelled from behind.

It was then that I heard it.

For the first time.

The river.

It was somewhere behind us, deep, deeper into the woods where there was neither sun of yellow nor leaf of green.

When I turned myself around, I felt myself alone.

Others soon followed me out of the coolness.

When we emerged, we were pale and ashen.

When I walked into the classroom, Miss Martin asked if I was all right.

I just smiled. She tried but failed to smile as she used to after she said, "The Father...loves the little children who come unto him."

I had heard it.

The black river.

The whooshing sound was like a pregnant ebony that never afterward disappeared from my sky.

To My Daughter

When I die you must

Come with me to the water's edge

Until the bell,

Until it rings

And I swim away

When I die you must come with me

Into the forest,

Gently watch as I climb the tree

When I die, we will go together

Into the Land of Nod

Embrace

Until you hold my heart

Until you feel the beat no more

Ursula

Little brat, skinny brat—I hear her tripping up the stairs, six-year-old friend of my darling Delphine.

"You little bitch," I felt like saying. I knew I would say that as soon as she opened the door. "You little bitch." I had closed the door like a coffin lid: glowing child prostrate, soon to be prostrate with my poison, the poison of rage.

Is that her stopping on the stairs to the second floor, is that her still trying to fix the merry-go-round horse I smashed like stained glass against the kitchen floor below? Minutes before she had opened her four-toothed mouth and laughed wildly at me as I sat eating my morning favorites: freshly baked doughnuts. Six of them. In neon light.

When she saw me eating, she said, I was like a giant. She emitted a snort from lips as large as lizards, a mouth infected with fleas. I said nothing. I only took the pretty horse she was holding and crashed it into a field of brokenness and pain. I stared at her with flashing knives for eyes. My anger, only now fully risen from the dead, sat beside me. Alive but mute.

Minutes later I wait here for the bitch to finish climbing the ladder of heaven: in this world the only ladder that skinny dolls with skinny mothers can climb.

I crack the door open. She stares my way. "Delphine!" she cries to my own little one. "Delphine! Now I know why your mom is obese! She ate six whole doughnuts for breakfast while I watched." Estelle guffawed till her teeth flew out of her mouth. She caught them, one by one, in hilarious hands of mean.

Estelle opened the lid of her own coffin wide: she snorted and charged into the second-floor room.

Anger, my alive but mute friend, nodded my way. It was time. I seized Estelle. I tore her hair: long, blonde, glimmering with pieces of moon. I tore it from her head in chunks. I pinched her cheeks: fresh as apples. Until the red flowed. I pushed her against the wall. Hard.

When I was through with her, Estelle looked like a doll, head cocked and fallen.

Then the alarm bell rang. It was a cry of the lamb.

I attended that sound. It was a sacred noise. The only one of its kind that I knew.

"Delphine!…Delphine!" I shouted.

"Coming, Mama!" Delphine's answer came from her bedroom on the second floor where she was still getting dressed for the day.

My darling appeared. She looked aghast at my wildly wailing victim. Delphine took my face in her hands. She looked into my eyes, "Please, Mama. You've done it before. I don't see it. I never see it. But give it to me, please."

I gazed upward into blue. And I waited.

Then, when the sun rose the next morning, I handed over my fierce companion. Delphine took the heavy round rage in both her hands and swallowed it whole.

I began to weep. Delphine kissed my neck and hands. She surrounded my bulk with her tiny fingers. She embraced me. She hugged me as only Delphine can do.

"Hush, Mama," she said.

"My darling, my mama."

I wept until the end of morning.

Like a polar bear covering her eyes, I hung my head in shame.

Contemporary Stories of Adults and Children

Ashes in an Urn

At first Bruce was busy at school, and happy. He was an extraordinary boy, not only an A student but captain of the bowling team and first flutist in the school orchestra. He painted, too (watercolor), and wrote poetry.

He was a good boy. He always followed the rules. He was a good Catholic boy.

I told him no steady girlfriend until he was twenty-one.

"Whatever you say, Mom."

I told him girls would be nothing but trouble until he was old enough to marry—that would be when he graduated from college and found a job. "You can date at sixteen," I said, "but make it clear to the girls from the beginning it is not going to be serious. Play the field. Encourage your girlfriends to, too. No sex until marriage. You learned that at church, didn't you?"

Bruce nodded. He answered, "It's the Lord's will."

Bruce was a good Catholic boy; he followed all the rules.

My Bruce was handsome. He was also sensitive and very shy: still, he was popular. According to my instructions, he started dating when he was sixteen. "Only on weekends," I said.

"Sure, Mom."

We had the same high expectations of our other children—a ten-year-old boy and a twelve-year-old girl. They weren't as easy to manage as their older brother. It was Bruce I had high hopes for.

One Saturday when he was sixteen and a half, Bruce brought home a girl from his bowling team. She was not just pretty. She was gorgeous.

I told him when he brought a girl home to keep her in the family room where they could watch TV, play the video games he and I had picked out together, or work on homework. It seemed to me they were doing fine. Bruce knew the rules; they did nothing but kiss. I only checked on them twice.

Dana was the girl's name. I invited her to dinner that evening. She smiled, made a call to her mom—whom I asked to talk to. It turned out Dana's family went to the same church as we did. The mom and I had a very friendly conversation.

And Dana stayed.

The whole family seemed to like her. I know I did. Bruce walked Dana to the door when dinner was over. I don't remember hers, but his eyes were glowing. Aglow in a way I had never seen them before. Not even on Christmas—his favorite holiday.

Bruce was a good boy. He followed the rules.

A year later something happened, something totally unexpected.

Bruce shot himself.

"Two months ago, I told him it was getting serious," Dana told me at the funeral. "Neither of our parents want this. And it makes sense!!! Besides, I'm dating someone else now. You need to play the field, too! Remember? That was our plan. We can still be friends.

"He told me then that if I left him, it would be like the Church leaving God or God leaving the world. There would be no point in living.

"I thought it better not to see him again after that. The conversation had become scary. After a few weeks of not seeing him, his terrifying words no longer haunted me!"

I was amazed at Dana's composure. Despite Bruce's death, Dana's heart seemed whole. I wondered how long she had reciprocated his feelings. Maybe she never did.

I was the first to find Bruce's body. It was lying in the garage, his dad's gun next to his head, and a note in his pocket:

"This is all we are without love: ashes in an urn."

Billie and John-y

Whenever Mom and Dad speak to one another—not often anymore—I plug my ears. Even little John-y gets scared. He's been crying a lot. I hear he's starting to slap other kids at preschool. He's only three—but even he knows something isn't right.

Yesterday Mom said John-y and I will be living with her. But whenever we hear from Dad, he says soon we'll be living with him.

This morning Dad told me Mom is a liar and not to listen to her, especially when she contradicts what he says.

In the evening I told Mom I have a book report due. I reminded her that Dad usually helps me when one comes due.

"I'll help you this time, sweetheart," she said.

"Dad publishes books for a living, you just teach them. No one loves books like Dad does."

"On second thought, Billie, I just remembered that tonight Dad and I are going to talk about setting a court date. I'll get a babysitter who can help you with your schoolwork. I know getting you a sitter is rare. But we're in an emergency situation."

"You were lying. Just now you said you were going to help me yourself."

"I wasn't lying, I just hadn't thought it through."

I stared at her.

"Can you get Sally Firona? She helps Joey with his homework. He says she knows a lot."

"I'll see what I can do."

"How do I know I can believe you? Dad says you lie all the time."

"Billie, Dad is telling you that you can't believe me because he's the one none of us can trust. Your dad has been having an affair since the time John-y was one. I only just recently found out. Once I got proof, I felt I knew him for the first time. He's a liar and a cheat!"

"I already know about the affair, Mom. Dad said if you hadn't spent so much time at work and with both of us kids, if you'd found more time for him, he wouldn't have had to have a relationship with someone else. He wants his new girlfriend to care for us full time. She doesn't have a job and she says she is more than happy to get a babysitter for us whenever he asks her to."

"That's because she's not going to care about you like I do. I'm your mother!"

"You wouldn't even get sitters so you could spend more time with Dad? I don't understand."

"Sweetheart, children are a family priority. In fact, children are what make a family. You're in school all day and Dad and I work all day. It's important to be together in the evening and on weekends. It's our only family time! Regular babysitters would have split us apart a long time ago."

"Dad doesn't see it that way."

That was the day the real pain started. That was the day I realized Mom will continue to say one thing and Dad another. That was when I recognized deep down: they don't love each other anymore. I could call Joey and ask what divorce was like for him; so what if he never wants to talk about it? But, no matter what Joey says, I have decided one thing: I don't want to live anymore.

"Mom, does this mean divorce?"

"You know it does, Billie. That's why Dad and I need to go to court. Because of what your father has done."

"But I love Dad! And I love you! You two are my whole life! Can't you find a way to stay together?!"

Mom stared at me.

And then I cried.

I cried until tears would not come anymore.

Mom hugged me but she kept silent.

Later that night, after she put John-y to sleep, Mom came into my room to say good night. She didn't say anything about Dad or the court date. And I didn't ask her.

"Have you heard of Jude the Obscure by Thomas Hardy? It was the book I did my report on tonight."

"Hardy has an awfully large vocabulary for a sixth grader."

"It's one of those Ready Read things that are short versions of longer novels."

"I didn't know about that series, but, yes, I know Hardy; in fact, I've taught that particular novel to my college students."

"Do you remember the part where the older boy—they call him Father Time—kills himself and his little step siblings, so he won't make life such a burden on the parents?"

"He wanted to help his parents out because of their poverty. They didn't need the extra mouths to feed."

"That's right!"

"It's nothing like our situation, Billie! You seem to think it is. We're not poor, we're just the opposite!"

"But, Mom, just like Father Time John-y and I have caused the problems between you and Dad, haven't we? Isn't it all our fault?"

"Billie, this has nothing to do with you kids—it's a problem between Dad and me."

"I don't believe you. Dad said the same thing and I didn't believe him, either. If it weren't for us, Dad wouldn't have had the affair and you two could stay married! That's what this is all about and that's what his girlfriend is for—to solve the problem of John-y and me. We have become the problem of the house.

"You used to talk about that wedding picture on the mantelpiece all the time, Mom. Remember? Didn't you used to say how happy you and Dad were to be married? What's happened? What's the problem, Mom? It's John-y and me, isn't it? It is. I know it is."

"Honey, things aren't that simple."

Then she looked me sadly in the eyes but said nothing.

She hugged me.

As soon as I heard her bedroom door close, I began to murmur out loud what I had thought to myself earlier in the day, "I need Mom and Dad to love each other again. But they never will. Ever. I know. I wish I had never come into the world so that they could have life and not die. I don't want to live any more. Maybe sometime, maybe one night, maybe tomorrow night, I will fall asleep and not rise with the morning sun."

Boy with No Heart

My mother

My father

My brothers.

One two three four bodies

Burst into flame.

An old man in the sky,

On the moon,

Weeps tears of blood.

Red pours as if to moisten earth and fire.

I, sole survivor,

take a gun, aim at the heart.

I wake

I sweat

I shout in darkness.

For others: an innocent tree ripening with papaya or mango.

For me: hoary head, axed arm hanging from branches.

For some: tranquility reigns in dwelling of light.

For me: ghosts of Mama, Papa, Alhaji and Ali

Laugh, sing as I look up,

muted by impossibility.

I want to fight rebel boys, enemy children, even in this thing called peace.

I struggle with nurses who harrow me with their tears.

Pity fell out with my heart two years ago when I was twelve.

Adult soldiers taught me the reason and the way: REVENGE.

I, and other orphans, trained to load and fire machine-guns, to fight as automatically as the AR-15.

Cocaine doped me as I angrily shot the rebels—who slaughtered my family like pigs.

It was thrilling at times, thrilling as a night filled with the beat of thunder.

Now that peace has come, violence of war haunts.

But I also am bored—no rifle, daily terror, or excitement of victory.

No russle of revenge.

No comrades-in-arms.

I have become a soldier to the bone.

My mother, my father, and my brothers are gone.

Now my army is gone: instrument of retaliation.

I look up to the moon and I weep.

Bread, Water, Song

I know I'm not free. My parents aren't free either. Not the way white folks are.

Like other blacks, my parents can't vote. They aren't allowed to register. They told me that the few blacks who are, are asked really picky questions about parts of what's called the Constitution. Nobody can answer those questions, they said. Whites, on the other hand, register and vote easy and free, without impossible tests, simply because of the color of their skin.

White people have the better neighborhoods, the nicer houses, great pools, and fine schools. White people don't have to get off the sidewalk to let black folks pass. It's the other way around. Black folks are allowed to shop in whites' department stores, the only ones in town, but they aren't allowed to eat in them.

I grew up feeling small. Even now I feel small though I'm a tall fifteen-year-old boy. I'm intelligent, too. I always get the highest marks in my classes, but still I feel inferior. Yes. My whole young life I've eaten the bread of humiliation, drunk the water of hurt, sung a tune of constant sorrow. It is because of them, those men and women who view us as not quite human, because we have skin (yes, it is black) and they are skinless (it has no color—they call it white). We have a sense of shame and they do not. We know right from wrong. They do not. We know what injustice is. They do not.

The Reverend Shuttlesworth is pastor at the Bethel Baptist Church in Birmingham, Alabama. In August of this year, 1957, two daughters of Reverend Shuttlesworth were trying to go to an all-white high school in Birmingham. They call it trying to integrate a school. I saw what happened on TV. I was overwhelmed by the viciousness of the white attackers—they tried to attack not only the two children but also the reverend himself and his wife. The mother was stabbed in the hip. The reverend was beaten with chains. Believe it or not, the reverend looked just like the reverend at our church here in Little Rock, Arkansas. Both he and his wife had to be taken to the hospital for their injuries. They had only been walking their two older children, Ricky and Pat, to a high school that was known for the wonderful knowledge it delivered. It was as simple as that. Or should have been.

I was traumatized by what I saw. I must have looked like a spook. My mom said, "Are you okay, son?"

At first, I didn't answer.

"Are you okay?" she insisted.

"No, Mom. How can I be okay when the lives of my brothers and sisters are being threatened? I feel their trauma in my own body, in my own bones. I feel it in my flesh, my blood."

Because of the fire that burned inside me from that night, the night I was shaken with sympathy and outrage, I volunteered to become one of a group that came to be called the Little Rock Nine. My mom and dad both work for white folks. They don't want to lose their jobs, so I get no encouragement from them. However, they don't actively discourage me, either. Maybe, secretly, they are proud of my actions. That is what I tell myself.

The Little Rock School Board told us that we nine would integrate grades 10–12 of Little Rock's Central High School, a school that has new and better books, better equipment, better facilities of all kinds that will help set our minds free in the way that our black school, Horace Mann, cannot. Central High is a public school, and it is our right to attend it. My pastor keeps telling me that and I listen. The reverend helps to give me courage.

Despite the threat of bayonets at first, later on, with the help of the troops sent by President Eisenhower, Central High was integrated in September 1957. Gradually, however, the troops began to leave. Now that we are left on our own, even the teachers are beginning to humiliate us, and not just by calling us "n****r" but by treating us as if we are dumb, not calling on us in class, no matter how often we raise our hands. Students call us with hate messages at home, they trip us up in the halls, pour water over us in gym class, ignore us in the cafeteria, refuse to sit in front or in back of us in the classroom.

As in many places before, here too I eat the bread of humiliation, I drink the water of hurt, I sing a tune of constant sorrow—but now I feel deep within my heart that this bread, this water, and this melody belong not just to me and other black people today, but to our ancestors, the slaves of the South. In my wounds I feel their wounds, in my spirit their spirit. And I know that it is through our suffering that we children, we too, we will overcome some day.

Dad the Artist

My dad was creative. He was only creative though when it came to me. On the other hand, he was pretty ordinary when it came to my two older half-sisters, whom I rarely saw but, as far as I know, he never harmed.

Dad used to love putting me in small spaces—he even built a tiny doghouse for me with a door that locked from the outside. He constructed it during the winter of the first year he was married to my stepmom. First, he took off all my clothes so he could watch me shiver from the cold. The temperature was subzero then in Northern Minnesota where we lived. He'd put me inside the hutch naked, without food or water. He let me crouch there for what seemed like an eternity but was probably one night and maybe part of a morning. At first, I howled and howled—like a dog—to be let out. "He was disobedient again," he would tell my new mother. "He needs a good punishment, so he'll learn to respect my rules." Dad put me in charge of cleaning the kitchen and the dishes in the evening, even though I was only five and a half years old. He always managed to find a dirty spot on a dish towel or a pea or small piece of meat on the floor. "Your housewife skills need work, Ned!" he cried and dragged me to the backyard for some "doghouse" time.

My stepmom, Tricia, didn't seem to care what my dad did. I later learned that she was so broken up about having lost her first husband to another woman, she was determined to hold on to my dad no matter what. She let him do whatever he wanted.

My actual mom had died in a car accident when I was four. Dad couldn't do without a woman so, the same year, he married Tricia, the good-looking divorcee next door who had often flirted with him. The woman had two teenage daughters who were rarely at home. They were always busy with school or visiting at friends' houses.

The key to my dad's torture of me was something that happened about a week into his new marriage. Dad found me in my stepsisters' room wearing a dress and carrying a purse. I also had lipstick on. My dad was furious when he saw me. He could see I was enjoying myself. "Faggot!" he yelled. He was not only furious but embarrassed, since I was his only natural child.

Tricia knew the real reason Dad punished me. But like him she thought gay people, especially gay boys, were an oddity. Nonhuman. When the two sisters learned about my sexual orientation from their mom, they didn't concern themselves. I don't think they even knew about the tortures that Dad put me through.

Dad liked to hang me upside down from the staircase for an hour or two. He would stuff my underwear in my mouth so I wouldn't cry out. He chose any torture that was unnatural, since he thought I was unnatural. I was a male who liked to act like I was female. I continued to dress in my sister's clothes whenever I could. The urge was something I couldn't resist. Pretending I was not a boy was the only thing in that house that brought me happiness.

Once Dad knocked out my teeth with a baseball bat so I couldn't smile at myself in the mirror when I put on girls' clothes. I vomited from the pain but also from shock when I saw what I looked like: blood instead of teeth. That was when Dad got real creative: he made me spoon my own vomit back into my mouth and sent me to bed without food. He smiled at me. "You've already had your dinner."

Sometimes when we were alone, Dad used me as a human ashtray. "Come on over here," he'd say. He took my shirt and T-shirt off. Whenever he was through with a cigarette—he smoked five or six of them while he sat there drinking—Dad would put his cigarette out on my chest. I cried out until he took out his belt. I knew what that meant and, as I learned to do in the doghouse, I became a statue and not a boy.

Dad and my stepmom were only together for two years. My dad left her for another woman, one who didn't know and, I assume, would never learn that he had fathered a gay boy.

At first my stepmom, who had been abandoned a second time now, wasn't sure what to do with me, but finally she turned me over to a welfare agency that put me in a foster home. Trish told the social workers I was gay and that she was not my biological mother. She also said she didn't want anything to do with me.

I found myself out on my own after years of running away from and being returned to foster homes where I was always persecuted for being who I was—

although never tortured as badly as my own father had tortured me. After a

while I found a decent job. There were many years of one-night stands until a man came into my life who became a steady partner.

How I endured the torment of my early years, I do not know. I began to wonder if the purpose of childhood, at least the childhood of someone who knows early in life that he is gay, was simply to learn patiently to accept whatever comes in hopes of someday being free. Sometimes it was impossible for me, though, to see a rainbow emerging from the blinding rain of confusion and misery in which I lived.

In 1992, the year Stanley and I began living together, I took an informal night class in the basement of the United Church of Christ. Stanley didn't want to have anything to do with religion because of its negative stance on gay people.

The course was called Homosexuality and Society. As my dad had shown, and as I learned in that class, brutality can be very creative. Demonic parents and serial murderers have a surprising amount of creativity in common. John Gacy, for example, is known as the Killer Clown because at one time, especially at children's events, he dressed up as a clown and called himself Pogo. Later, during the murders, he'd use magic arts he had learned during his Pogo days to trick his victims into handcuffs. He sometimes stuffed a boy's underwear in the boy's mouth before he killed him, just as my dad had done with me when he hung me from the staircase. Gacy made $100,000 from his paintings while he was in prison. Many of them were images of clowns like Pogo. Gacy's artistry ended when he was executed for the murder of thirty-three male youths, most of whose skeletons were found buried beneath his home. At least a third of his victims were children.

Daddy

It Christmas Eve, fuckin Christmas Eve. You out there with your bell-bell lives, you dont know fuckin shit about hos like me—you think you do, with your judge-judge eyes, but what do you know? Think about it. What do you know?

You know about my mom who cant never—or almost never—get off heroin or coke? You know about her diseases in the head and in the heart? You know all about it, dont you?

You know about my dad, too? What there was of him. Mom says he was only with her and me for two years before he split. Now he in prison for pushin drugs.

How I made it to what age I am now, I couldnt tell you. I still a child, though. I aint never had what they call motherin or fatherin my whole life—least not till now.

What I do member is that one Christmas Eve when my mom told me to go out, to find a friend and have a good time. Well, I didnt want to leave her. It Christmas and she the only family I have. But I did it because she told me three times and I knew what that meant. Well, when I got home really late that night there was a note settin on the kitchen table. I got a really bad feeling in my stomach when I seen it. "I through, baby, I through." And then she put a little heart there, she got a crayon and colored the heart red. Thats the night I found her dead upstairs. Overdose. Shed done it befo, but it worked for her this time.

Dont feel bad for me, you judge-judge trash out there—you aint never felt bad for me befo, have you?

Well, dont feel bad for me now, cause my dad may be in jail and my mom may be dead, but after I run away from two foster homes, I found myself a real dad, my Daddy who cares for my ass like nobody I ever knowed. He forty-five and I am thirteen—he old enough to be my daddy and young enough to be my lover.

Long as I bring him money—he thinks its shit I aint white, though he aint, either. He'd be makin more money if I was, he says—but as long as I bring home regular money, he treat me sweet.

Usually says I too dumb to know what to do with the money myself. I proud to say I do have a fifth-grade education—from LA School Distric, too! I told him so—I was smart in school—still he say I a dumb ho who aint got no real smarts, aint got a brain in my fuckin head, he say. I guess I beginning to believe him. I am pretty stupid. But I told him I was smart enough to go with him when he found me sittin on a curb in Hollywood. I was smart enough to do that. I was smart enough to believe him when he said if I came with him, hed treat me good. Smart enough to accept the really cute clothes he bought me then. I smart enough to get into the life where I have a Daddy who cares—as long as I bring in stash regular since I dont make too much cause of the color of my skin. Still, I real young. He liked that and so do all the johns what hover round me every night.

One of them white bitches came to my door the other day when Daddy was out—she a wife-in-law, cant tell you how much I hate her ass. One look at her and I punched her in the jaw. I punched her in sort of the way Daddy punches me when I dont make enough for him—or sometimes just because he says thats what my stupid ass deserves when I dont obey him and all his rules. In some ways maybe I do deserve it from him. It calm me down and I learn to obey better. Its like an act of love when he do it. Well, it werent no act of love from me to her. I punched her so hard, she started to scream. Then I slammed the door. You could hear her whimperin really bad out there. I told her I never want to see her motherfuckin face again! So what if she sleep with my sun, too? So what? That sun, he shine only for me. He tells me so. Regular.

When daddy and me make love—especially when he do it the regular way— everything turn out okay. Then I forget all the bad parts and just remember the good—like I did for a while with my mom when—every once in a while—she got off or at least wasnt on heroin or crack.

Like I say, my Daddy—he take care of me—unlike my real daddy who I wouldnt even recognize if I seen him. It been so long.

You creepy people with the judge-judge eyes, though—theres plenty o sufferin in a life like this one—aint much different from the life I run from—at home where nobody was there for me—or in foster homes where there so many kids those people dont even know, yet I bet I dont run away. You must think I'm stuck.

I aint stuck.

I just in a different life where theres my Daddy who I see just bout every day. He bring me Hershey chocolates—especially after we just have a big fight—but like I tol you, its the good I remember. He says I love you regular, you know that something completely new and star-like for me.

Sides, we got pretty good money and all cause I go out there at night and spread my legs. That aint too hard, is it? Not for a regular life like the one I got.

It took three hours and it cause lots of horble pain, but Daddy made the tattoo person he knows tattoo my butt with Daddys Bitch written in laborate white. I shrieked pretty bad with that. But like when he punch me, I come to the conclusion that it good for me, after all. In fact, I proud of it now, because it shows how special I am to him. He didnt do this to any of the other wifes-in-law. I know he didnt. I the youngest and the cutest of the bunch—even if my skin is black and not white.

At least this Christmas I got somebody steady to share it with. He aint going to kill himself and he aint going to leave me.

I bet he going to bring home something special tonight—he said he was—might be champagne. I hopin so!

I a lucky girl even with all my bruises and broken bones from the johns and from Daddy, too—Daddy even tried to choke me once. That was bad stuff. But turned out okay. At the end he said he couldnt go through with it. That because he love me deep down. I know he do.

It not so bad being a girl, a black girl like me.

You judge-judge people out there, dont you feel sorry for me now. Yo. I live the life. I aint never lived it before.

Everything else, including you out there, everything else is square.

My Daddy teached me that.

I aint square like you.

All because I let my Daddy find me when I sittin there despairin on the curb in Hollywood cause I had nowhere to go.

He my one, my Daddy is.

He my god.

He my one and only luv.

He it.

So, what you make of these here tears rollin down my cheeks? You out there, livin your bell-bell lives.

I wipin them away fast as I can so Daddy wont see me when he walk in that door.

If he see me cryin, he punch me first thing. He hate tears—specially mine.

He comin in, I know he is, with a bottle o bubbly. I sure he will tonight.

It Christmas Eve.

Geezis

Never knew how glorious the white was. Or the cold. Or the sight of the rabbit my uncle once caught, cooked, and ate by himself around the fire in our igloo. Never knew how beautiful it was to eat ordinary caribou by his side on that night.

Didn't know the warmth of my grandmother's stories. I was ignorant that they were my deepest embraces. I took for granted Grandma's love, my mother's, little sister's.

I lived for the hunt, hunting with other men, including my father. I was unaware of our magnificence. Loved but didn't know. I loved nature and the things of nature. Loved but didn't know. I loved the Great Spirit who, I was taught, created all.

Didn't know any of these things until someone came and took them away.

Men from the Canadian government kidnapped me and took me to a school run by nuns. Or was it a prison? And were the instructors with crosses hanging from their necklaces, were they guards?

It was 1959 when this happened.

I will always remember how my grandmother shrieked, tears streaming, as I left the igloo, never to return. She and I both knew I would never return. My older brother had been taken years earlier and none of us had ever seen him again.

One dark day, glowing with the morning sun, I left behind all mystery: mystery of family, of belonging, of kinship. The mystery of the Great Spirit. All the glories of the world, a world I called my own, were taken from me on that day.

First my handsome long black hair was cut.

"No Ojibwe!" "Speak only English! You will learn your new language soon enough. You will thank us—you heathens, you half-breeds. We will make you Christians. We will make you white in spirit."

We each had one book—a Bible they called it. We stayed on one page, until the "Our Father" became a part of us—or so they thought. It was all strange to me. I learned to read but I was a slow reader, a slow learner. I earned as many whippings as anyone in the class for what one nun called the crawling quality of my mind.

When the Residential School first took me in, I was ten years old. Five years of routine chores and learning, mostly religious subjects. A little free time was given us, though, too, when we could go outside, play games, and be with nature for a short while.

Five years of this routine and then a foster family asked to complete my way to whitehood, to Christianity. From what the family and the nuns whispered to the foster parents, when I first met them, I understood that the government paid good money to the family to finish my "education."

The mom and dad—they had two grade-school-aged children—chose a high school for me. It was Catholic, like the Residential School where the nuns both taught and punished me for not being like them.

No matter how "white" I acted or spoke I could never actually be white. I was Indian to the bone. Sometimes when I was walking with my new family to church, someone across the street would say, "Hi Geronimo!" or "Where's your horse and your long hair, Tonto?" People everywhere, even in my foster family, when they were mad at me for something, they sneeringly called me "half-breed."

There were a few blacks there at the white school, but not a single person of my own kind.

I was always alone.

One day, though, I joined the basketball team. They were always looking for good players—they didn't care that I was Indian. I had always liked playing the sport during free time at the Residential School. And I was good at the game, I knew I was.

The boys saw I was talented, the coach, too. I was unusually tall, tallest among them, so I played center. For the first time since I left my natural family, I felt a touch of humanity coming my way, a touch of belonging. Some were jealous of my height and my skill. But once they saw I just enjoyed the sport and didn't care about what others thought, they stopped bullying me.

My junior and senior year, after we won a game, we would drink. I loved the effect of drink. When I drank too much, though, I became depressed. It was strange that this could happen when I was celebrating my happiness with a newfound "gang" of friends.

The beautiful and vast stretches of natural white I had taken for granted, the land and rivers where Dad and I hunted, the warmth of my grandmother's stories, the love of my mother and little sister would not fade. The vision was like an unattainable heaven to me. It always appeared to me in deep drink. The apparition was so beautiful my heart became sad and sore.

My foster family fed me, took me to church, gave me a place to bathe and sleep. But that was all. The dad was never there. The family was poor, and he always worked overtime. He basically blanked out on weekends. He wanted to be left alone. The mother, although you could see she cared for me, was always too busy to spend time: she was a full-time grade-school teacher and a parent and a housekeeper, too. About every third weekend, she took me and the other two children, six and seven years old, on an outing with her. But that was all. Given the circumstances, it was impossible for a personal relationship to develop between us. It was the same with the kids—given their young ages.

My basketball team slapped me on the back when I made a difficult basket. We sang together on the bus as we went from school to school to play ever more challenging teams, And the booze really flowed when we won a tournament.

However, it would all be finished when high school was over. I didn't even interview for a basketball scholarship to college, and no one encouraged me to make the effort. It was all right, though. I had always known I wasn't college material.

I was good with my hands. I decided I wanted to become an apprentice. My goal was to become a carpenter.

When I started carpentry, I was still Jesus, what the nuns at the Residential School had named me. Not Geezis, as I was born. They tried to make Christian names as close to Indian names as they could. Geezis is "the sun" in Ojibwe. The last time I was called "sun" or Geezis was the morning the white man took me from the igloo. It was my grandma calling me back to her and our way of life.

Recently, at eighteen, I did go back to see the place where I had first lived. I did not recognize it. I saw no people I had called Grandma or Mother or Sister. No men with whom I hunted, including my father. On that day I could not feel the presence of the Great Spirit. Where had He gone? Father, Son, and Holy Spirit had never taken root in my heart. No matter how hard the nuns had tried to beat the new religion into me, I had no creator, no God to whom I could pray, in whom I could believe. If there was a God, He had abandoned me.

I sat along the shore of the lake where my family had lived and took a bottle of whiskey from my back pocket. I imagined a kind of paradise was available to me here on earth, through the bottle.

Alcohol became my best friend because of what it helped me to believe. I knew the object of my new faith was a mirage, but I didn't care. I saw what whiskey had done to other Ojibwe. It killed them. It would probably kill me, too. Maybe it had taken my older brother away forever, the one who was kidnapped and who had never come back to us.

Maybe from my coffin—just maybe—I will actually go back to this other world, the Indian world, the one place I can call home.

I Am Mother

I am Mother. The Mother of all.

I hear the children as they call, "Mama! Mama!"

I hear as they cry their wounds:

Their wounds from the battlefield.

O children, do not cry to me!

This month, this very month—July 2016—I have heard shouts from South and West Chicago.

No, my darlings:

Do not shout to me.

I hear the tiny soldiers as they fall:

A child's jaw is fractured, a little one's lung pierced. I weep as a small torso becomes paralyzed from the waist down: debilitated for long life.

On the Fourth of July I see two children's legs shot through. Shattered not by fireworks but by bullets, bullets meant to kill.

All in one month: victims aged three to eight.

My heart is large.

Larger than the mountains or the sea.

But my heart hits a roadblock when it walks onto the battlefield.

I take up the wounds of the young, I nurture, and I heal.

But I am impotent, I am powerless to prevent war wounds; nor can I make them vanish.

I rest here with a weak, a flabby heart.

No, little ones, do not look to me to solve your pain.

I suffer only, I wield no wand.

No, my treasures:

Do not look to me.

Jesus before Pilate

I was delighted when Father Paul, pastor and religion teacher at St. Matthew's, took an interest in me. A personal interest. I needed it.

My father, to whom I had been close, had just died after a six-year illness. My mother was a hopeless alcoholic. She had been in and out of rehab two times since my father began his battle with cancer. Each time my dad and I had hope. But to no avail.

I was in the seventh grade when my friendship with Father Paul began. I was an altar boy. Religion meant everything to me—religion and the priest I was growing to love. Father was charming. He was also affectionate. He took me to the church during off-hours. He explained the stained-glass windows, the stations of the cross, the statues, the messages in Greek and Latin above the church doors. I can't tell you how attached I became to him during those private lessons. Paul was my priest and my friend. He was my one true thing.

One evening, we went into the church and he actually let me sit on the altar! Then he sat next to me, like we were buddies. He hugged me. And I hugged him. I almost told him I loved him. But I was afraid.

It was hot that evening. He took off his shirt. He looked me in the eyes and said, "You're lonely, aren't you? I am, too. That's why we need God. God wants us to be together." I could hardly believe what I was hearing. I was ecstatic.

He asked me to remove my shirt. I did. This excited me. I felt close to him. He stroked my hair. Then my shoulders. I trusted him. He was my teacher. He was my priest.

He picked me up and lay me down on the altar and he took off his pants. "This is all a part of God's plan, Cecil. It's all part of God's loving plan for us."

He smiled his beautiful warm smile and then he asked me to take off my pants. I did so. He picked me up again and turned me over on my stomach.

Then he thrust a part of himself inside me. I cried out. "Stop!" I said. "Stop! Please stop!" But he didn't seem to hear me. He was groaning with pleasure. Then, suddenly, there was silence.

I was bleeding from behind. He said it was like Jesus bleeding on the cross. And that I would be okay. He gave me an altar towel. "You need to be alone now, alone to pray." And then he left.

I tried to call him back. I tried again and again. But I was too weak: I fainted.

When I came to myself, the bleeding had stopped. Time passed. I couldn't stop crying.

I went out into the darkness. I called his name.

In response, a cold star shone in the sky.

God also. God was silent.

From that day forward I belonged to the priest—no matter how much confusion and pain he caused. I let him do whatever he wanted with me. And wherever he wanted to do it. Besides hating him, you see, I loved him. And only him. There was no one else in my life. In addition, I couldn't have spoken the unspeakable to anyone.

It was younger boys he needed to train in Christ's sacrificial love. And when I turned fifteen, he said, I had been fully trained. He moved on. He moved to a different parish.

When he left me, I was more lonely than I had ever been. I began to think of him as Judas Iscariot.

"Whatsoever you do to the least of my brethren, that you do unto me."

Over the years my adult relationships with both women and men have fallen apart one by one. I was married and had a little boy once, but I felt alien from him, and when my wife divorced me, she took full custody. I had no objection. It was better for the boy. I do not want any more children.

When I was in my early forties, I found the parish where Father Paul was assigned to at that time. "I am Cecil." I said to him. "Remember me?" Then helplessly and hopelessly I said what I had come to say, "You have annihilated my life."

Astonished, he looked at me. He said nothing.

My God also has forsaken me. I live in a black reservoir, a dark hole haunted by a figure climbing down from the cross.

Like a Shotgun

The color of our skin, our ethnicities weren't all the same. But we were all people of color and we all lived in neighborhoods that bled poverty.

We were all children too—ages fourteen to sixteen. The sixteen-year-old felt like he was twelve because he had hearing difficulties and learning disabilities.

Because we were so young, we needed our families. We needed to have them with us, especially when questioning became brutal. Some of us had a relative with us, some did not. As youngsters we did what our family members told us to do—we knew they were on our side. That was all that mattered. We were all, adults and children alike, under the impression that if we lied to the cops, we would be let go. If we confessed to something we didn't do, the gates to home, nearly closed now, would open wide. The shedding of integrity could be traded for safety and warmth. That's how the system seemed to work.

But we were deluded; we never did go home—just a few of us, and only for a while, on bail. We all went to trial, and we all went to jail because we had confessed. We had thought, wrongly, that the confessions would liberate us. The prosecutor had no hard facts, but she had our admissions of guilt. So what if the details each of us gave didn't agree with one another? We made up different stories about how we had assaulted and raped the white lady in Central Park. She was in the hospital for quite a while, though she eventually was let go.

It seemed to make a big difference to the cops—and to the people of New York City, once they heard—that the woman who was raped was white and not black or Latino like us. They made it a race crime. They wanted to make a race thing out of it. And they wanted us—the Central Park Five they called us—to be the rapists. They wanted it like a baby boy wants his milk. Those white people needed us to be guilty. So they saw that it happened. Tears come when we think about how they used us like a shotgun to kill our innocence of the crime. What they killed was our childhood. What was left of it.

We all maintained our innocence when we came up for parole. Lies had gotten us into jail; the truth kept us there. There is no skin color attached to a false or a true statement. This was a fact we learned through our experience with prison.

One of us couldn't go to juvenile jail because he was older than the rest. He was sixteen. In his prison—Rikers—he was told by an inmate that all five of us were innocent. This guy knew because he himself had raped and assaulted the white lady in the park. At that time, he was in jail for other crimes.

The sperm of this guilty serial murderer and rapist matched the sperm that was contained in the white jogger's rape kit. None of our sperm had matched it. That key fact hadn't mattered to the prosecutor any more than the forced quality of our confessions did. The district attorney had been well aware of both.

When the evidence stared people in the face, we were finally cleared of the crime. Most of us had been physically freed after seven to ten years of prison, but then we were known for having a criminal past. That made life hard. Now that our innocence was made known, opportunities opened for jobs and schools and relationships that had been closed before. We were even well compensated for the injustice that had been done. We were not the same, though, even then. No amount of money could make up for lost years of freedom. The late years of childhood—high school life and the love of any family that we had. Those years had been taken from us. Our souls had been ripped apart.

No. Money didn't matter. It was the hole inside our heart that mattered. The hole that never was and never could be filled. That rupture, a spiritual one, we endured for the rest of our lives.

Ma and Pa

Flash of light, period of darkness, frame after frame pass in mid-dream...

I boarded an orphan train in 1915 when I was eight years old. I left my mother, who was dying of tuberculosis, and my drunken father behind in New York City. I was headed to Missouri. I would never see my ma or pa again. Although neither was ever far from my dreams. Even if they couldn't provide for me, they were still my ma and pa. The Children's Aid Society told me to forget my parents. They even took away from me a leather bracelet that my dad had given just before I was put into the New York Foundling Hospital. Inside he had lovingly though stumblingly incised my name: Erin Pickett.

"You are all going to new homes now. Good clean religious homes out West. Forget your families, if you have any. They could not support you, so they are dead to you. You are about to begin a new and disciplined and upright life with a new couple who will choose you from the crowd. They will be your real parents."

At our first stop in Browning, Missouri, I stood on stage with ten other children. We had been spruced up for the occasion. Adults looked us over like we were cows for their cattle yards.

"There's a smart-looking one down there," I heard a woman say. "Let's get her for the housework and baby care. What do you say, Frank?"

"Okay, Katie. But we've got to get home before the blizzard begins."

They signed the paperwork.

At first, I liked having my own room and eating at a full table, neither of which I had known before—either at my real home, a one-room dwelling where some form of starvation was all we ever knew, or the orphanage, where we were given a bed and just enough food to keep us alive.

Mr. and Mrs. Mulroy had three children and a fourth on the way. I didn't know what was going to be expected of me. I was so tense throughout dinner on that first evening, I could not speak.

Though my duties for the couple actually went okay for a couple of weeks, they soon became worse. I couldn't sleep because the children—all very little—cried in the night and I was always expected to settle them. Besides, Mrs. Mulroy had a habit of beating me when she felt I hadn't cleaned the kitchen properly. As my health began to fail, I became more and more careless with my chores. In fact, I came down with pneumonia and nearly died.

When the agent for the Children's Aid Society came to check on me, he realized he was going to have to find a different place. As soon as I was well enough, he took me from the Mulroys to the O'Briens, who were only ten miles away. Once again, I had my own room. This one was on a farm, and my place had a beautiful view of the fields. The farmer and his wife asked me to feed and watch the hogs and chickens every day. Eventually they had me helping the hired farm workers to pick corn. I also went on any errand they assigned.

I thought I did my work well, but the O'Briens were never satisfied. And like at the Mulroys, here too I was treated like a servant, not a daughter. They wanted work out of me, an almost unbearable amount, and nothing more. They treated me well enough to keep me alive for my tasks. But that was all.

After a year, I began to ask myself nearly every day, "Why not leave?"

It was about a year after that when I decided I couldn't take it anymore. The couple's indifference to me had become unbearable.

I was beginning to give up on "family life," whatever that was.

During those last nights at the O'Briens, I began to dream of my ma and pa. I cried out to them in the darkness. I would wake up in a fever of anguish and confusion.

Once, when I had walked into town, I met an elderly childless couple who owned the shop where I was buying candles for the O'Briens. I talked to the couple, and they said they would pay me for work I could do for them if things got really bad at my "home." I told them I had been placed there by the Children's Aid Society and couldn't just leave.

This shop was where I ran to, a bag of clothes and supplies in tow. The name of the owners was Smith. I stayed with them for four years. They weren't Irish like me or like the other two couples I had been lodged with, but what did that matter compared to the wages they would provide? They hired me right away and let me sleep in their back room. My bedroom was very small—like a closet—but I had good meals every day. Apparently, the Children's Aid Society had forgotten me. I was glad. Here I was valued, treated kindly, and allowed indulgences from time to time like an ice cream on a hot afternoon or a penny candy for dessert on a holiday.

Then the Depression came. The Smiths were forced to let me go. They gave me what bonus they could. I was touched when they wept as I left. I cried, too. They were the closest I had ever come to feeling loved.

I was fifteen and knew that I was—as always—dispensable. All I had was my bonus and what I had saved from my earnings over the years.

No roots. No home. No family.

Twenty-five dollars would last me a while, but then...I would be back on the human train.

Flash of light, period of darkness, frame after frame pass in mid-dream...

I envision my ma and pa.

Magnum Opus

The great Norwegian murderer of seventy-seven victims, Anders Breivik, taught me that *Modern Warfare 2* is the best trainer's video for a massacre, for any military goal I want to undertake—solo. I have used it well. I have turned it into artistry—self-expression. In the process, I found for the first time in my life a community that welcomes me: this mostly adult group of killers who love arms and mass murderers, just as I do.

Mom gave me the equipment to bring my video existence to real life—real guns of all kinds. Connecticut law says twenty-one is the legal age for firearms. I am twenty, but for a man on an artistic mission—and for my mother's son—laws do not apply.

My mission has descended.

I have accepted it. Words do not work for me. Not with my diseases—Asperger's (time and again social interaction eludes me) and a sensory-processing disability (I abhor being touched but cannot feel pain). I have been creating sketches of the dead and dying since the fifth grade to express how I feel about life as I live it. No one looks at them. They are not enough to convey to the world the fright, the dread, the rage inside me.

In high school Mr. Novia, the computer instructor, knew that I was the only student who could build a computer from scratch. I was the supreme techy. He cared for me, too, besides admiring me. For example, he knew I would withdraw completely from the world, quit society, if I ever left the school. This worried him, as both Mom and I could tell. But Mom pulled me out of Newtown High anyway when Novia changed his job—she hated the place as much as I did—except for this man whom we both had trusted but who betrayed us by leaving when I needed him like a dad.

Eventually I had no friendships, no relationships, no family. The last I let go was my mother, the only person in whom, for years, I had confided. Affection is hard for me, almost impossible with my touch disease. I left my father once he started seriously dating other women: his and mom's divorce made life hell on Earth for me. And I left my uncle (the Marine I idolized as a kid), and my brother, Ryan. I did all this when my dad betrayed me completely by showing he wanted to marry again after what had been only an off-and-on separation from Mom.

I carried my mom's and dad's separation papers to school with me in my briefcase: that was about all I did take to school—no one seemed to notice, though. Or care. Of course, I was a loser. Everyone knew that. Even me.

The changing of classes that began in middle school was special torture for me: I can't stand change of any kind of light or noise.

Though I hated everything about school but the studies—I was quite good at those—there was one place where I almost felt comfortable: the shooting range. Mom gave me my first gun when I was four. First, we loaded and shot our guns together. Mom grew up in gun territory—in the New Hampshire countryside. We had fun with our hobby for a number of years. Till one day she told me it would lead nowhere because of my sensory disease: "If you can't let anyone touch you, how can you be a Marine?"

After months of depression, I finally decided: if not the life of a Marine, then I will be an artist!

First, my mother. I find her in her bedroom. She told me that the world could not be mine, that I could not be a Marine: she is my first target on this my artist-made mission. She will not rob me of my destiny—she will be its first trophy! *Bam bam bam bam!* Blonde-haired bloody bitch!

Magnum opus.

Just begun.

Now, the whole of Newtown, Connecticut, will be my artist's canvas. To represent the village, I choose the school. I have finally arrived. But I see two cop cars in the parking lot of Newtown High. Careful!

Instead, I pull up to Newtown Grade School nearby. No policemen there. Students at this school were the first to make me feel my hopelessness, my outcast state. Kaynbred, my video persona, is tall and mighty, muscle-bound, not frail and skinny and given to trances like Adam Lanza was. Kaynbred is my man.

The massacre I trained myself for on video in my downstairs Dark Room (for years) is about to begin. No words will be needed: a work of art for the Newtown Art Museum. Now people will know, they will notice, and my creation will last for eternity. Weaponry is my mouthpiece: I have lived for this. By this I will express myself completely.

Magnum opus.

My creation will be splendid: the expression of despair and helpless rage completely beautiful—an unsurpassable aesthetic piece. Once again, no words: let the gun speak. The supreme beauty of perfect self-expression begins its reign. Now—

I just shot through the front window with the Bushmaster rifle, now I walk down the hall, then turn left into the first-grade room where my public humiliation began. *Bam bam bam bam*…fifteen schoolchildren dead. A pretty picture: white boots flying, green eyes flashing, multicolored dresses covered in blood. This part of my mission I have accomplished!

Now another first-grade room: like clay pigeons, five more tykes down—*bam, bam, bam, bam, bam*. Now twenty children plus six adults along the way—all strewn in blood, the artistic medium I choose.

Now for the *pièce de résistance*. The mission is about to be consummated! I take out the Glock handgun, a military pistol. Straight against my head: *BAM!*

Mutti

My days are consumed like smoke, and my bones are burned.

My heart is smitten and withered like grass.

I left Mutti seven years ago, when I lived with her in a foreign land, my homeland, my Deutschland.

Juden were no longer welcome there:

we were beaten

we were sent to prison

our temples were burned

they bound us and took us where we did not want to go.

There was glass everywhere.

Broken

As us, as the paths of our lives.

It was 1938. November 9.

Kristallnacht, they called it.

My father had been taken to a camp. We knew we would not see him again.

Mutti wanted to save me, little Hilda, her only child.

A neighbor showed us the way: *Kindertransport*.

When my mother packed for me, she hid two jewels in the heels of my shoes.

"I don't want to go to England, Mutti."

"You do want to go, liebschen. You will be safe there."

"I am only seven," I sobbed. "You and I are one. Would you break us for life?"

"I would. For your life. I will come. I will be with you very soon."

Next morning, very early, she took me to the train station. I saw my neighbor on the train. He was eight. I sat next to him.

As the train pulled out of the station, I waved to my mother and said, "See you very soon!"

I stopped crying for a time.

My new mother in England was kind to me. But I felt nothing for her.

I did what I was told. Fear was my guide in all things.

Fear and a longing I sensed every day would not be quenched.

No. Mutti did not come.

My days are consumed like smoke, and my bones are burned.

My heart is smitten and withered like grass.

My new mother and I began to hear news of the inferno: war at home, a war that had come to England.

We went north to Liverpool, my new mother and I, to escape the bombing in London. We lived with my new mother's sister for a year. Then we returned to our home.

"I will be with you very soon." These words still echoed in my ears.

Four years later the war ended. It was 1945.

"Your own mother," my new mother said, "she has been spared. She is on her way. She is coming from Germany. She survived the war!"

A few days later I heard my German mother say, "It is I. You have changed. You are no longer little Hilda! You are no longer my own girl. Get ready, whoever you are. We will go to Australia to be with your uncle. And we will go together."

"I am fourteen now. You are not my Mutti. I do not want to go with you. You said you would be with me soon. Very soon. But you lied to me, didn't you? I see that you are different now. You are broken. You are old. And ashen.

"No. I will not go with you. Whoever you are. I will stay here. I will finish school and find work. I don't love you or my English mother. My life stopped when my young, my beautiful Mutti sent me away. I was seven years old. She and I were one. The time for oneness is past. I see that now. It existed once and then it was shattered before its time.

"The jewels in my shoes: my two precious mothers whom I cannot love because you abandoned me. You disabled my heart when you made me leave on the train to England. You sent me where I did not want to go. I would rather have stayed and suffered with you than have left you as I did.

"But now I will find a man and I will marry him. We will have children of our own. And I will never…I will never make my children go where they do not want to go. I will allow them, if they love me, to stay by my side through storm and through thunder, through the flames to become ash with me, if that is what they choose."

My days are consumed like smoke, and my bones are burned.

My heart is smitten and withered like grass.

Omran, Mon Amour

The boy, only five years old, appeared one night between trashcans, eyes wide open, scared in alarm.

He was looking for a can, a country he could call his own.

The boy's face looked shattered in starlight.

The boy's hands glinted under the moon like glass weeping fast in the rain.

The boy's eyes were hollow like a drum; they were dead with despair like the displaced who were decimated by rise of war in the East.

His tiny body had been drowned three times, raised three times, then drowned again.

His little legs looked bewildered: they wore the weary mask of the dead.

His hair, covered in ash and dirt, lay motionless like a blanket for one hand.

His feet, I could hear his feet dancing to the tune of trumpets, trumpets of terror, swaying to songs of the sinister, waltzing to the final note of destruction: *Omran, my love, mon amour.*

Your brown face begins to fade like life as I search for you tonight. I hear no note of a delighted baby's wail.

Your stress hides naked in trash, huddling outside in cold tin cans.

Your face is set on fire by the light of bombs in war.

Blood drips in drops down child's cheeks, dead under siege.

No: your moaning did not cease when you turned phantom.

You are always with me, you, Omran, victim of masked men determined to assault squirming children of war, children of the world.

Rag Doll

Aisha's Aba used to have a large flock of goats from which he earned money to support his family. But there had been a drought lately and now his flock was too small to garner sufficient money. Even worse, a civil war had begun. Every evening, as the family sat down to their simple meal of beancakes, Aba prayed to Allah to keep his two wives and five children from harm.

One day Amal, mother of Aisha, came to her daughter and said that Bilal was going to save the family from poverty. Bilal, Aba's good friend, was going to pay a bride-price of 450,000 Sudanese pounds for the privilege of marrying Aisha. He quoted the famous line that Mohammed had married a nine-year-old girl and her name was Aisha. That money would help her parents to care for the baby and the three small boys. Not only that, but they would no longer have to feed Aisha, their little girl.

At her mother's words, Aisha looked scared. "Umi, I am too young! I am only nine—some people think I am eight or seven."

"Aba thought of your youth," she replied. "He made Bilal promise before Allah he would not take you until a year after your first period. You will be twelve or thirteen then."

"But I don't want to leave school—what about my poetry writing? And I can't leave my friends! They are my whole life."

"If you marry you will not go to school unless your husband approves. You know already that men make all the decisions and women obey them."

"But I am not a woman! I am a girl!"

"Yes, you are a girl right now. You are a child, and children obey their fathers. Once they are married, they obey their husbands. There is nothing you can do about this. It is a matter of honor, a matter of religion, here."

Aisha ran to her room, where she began to cry. Her mother came in to soothe her. She put her arm around her daughter. "You will get used to it. This will protect you from a dishonorable life, from being raped by violent men. Believe me, they are everywhere, especially now with the men at war in our own country. You will not only be safe, you will be well off—well housed and well fed. Bilal is a wealthy man. You are very lucky that he wants you!"

Although she was listening, Aisha covered her ears and pretended she was not. "Leave me, please! Leave me!" she kept shouting through her sobs. After her mother left, she cried herself to sleep.

When she awoke, all she could think about was Bilal. She had met him twice. Twice she had noticed his bad breath and his age and how fat he was. He was old enough to be her grandfather. He was fifty-five. Aisha couldn't believe her bad fortune. But she knew she had to accept it.

When she saw her friends at school, she said, "In two months I am to be married! And not to the man of my dreams, but to the man of my nightmares! The worst of all is I am leaving school and going to another family, and I must leave you two behind, you who are my happiness!"

When the fateful day arrived, Aisha had frightful visions of what would happen later that day. After a short wedding ceremony, she said goodbye to her family, and she went to Bilal's home.

Bilal already had one wife who came to greet her—she was about sixteen. Hisafa took Aisha to her room. "You will sleep here. Wash yourself and then come to my room, which is across the way." She smiled. Aisha liked her. She was gentle and pretty. And her own room was quite large and beautifully decorated. It began to look like things weren't going to be so bad after all.

By the end of the day Hisafa had explained the rules of the house to Aisha. She said it was especially important that the new bride should follow the rules: "That way you will make a good impression and maybe he will treat you well at night."

"Treat me well?" Aisha said in alarm. "He promised not to touch me for three or four years. I am only a child now."

Hisafa gave her a look that was not friendly. "Don't make him angry or the whole household will suffer."

After dinner, the child bride went back to her room.

Years later, when Aisha was asked by a woman lawyer to describe her experience with Bilal, she chose that first night to convey how she felt when he raped her. Though he continually assaulted her throughout her three years of legal bondage, that first night was the one she would never forget.

I left my clothes on that night.

My heart called to me.

Sleep came.

I woke to the echoing of my heart's call.

When I fell asleep again, beautiful blackness enfolded me.

Suddenly I felt naked: the light went on.

I saw him come toward me.

I smelled him as he came.

I was David to his Goliath.

Only I was a David out of favor with God.

He took off my clothes.

My heart was calling me.

I closed my eyes.

His stare: I could not see but I could feel it.

His gaze was raping me slowly.

He ate me like a fruit no longer forbidden.

My heart called to me.

An inner wind blew me apart.

I felt like a doll without arms or legs.

I wanted to scream, but he covered my mouth with his silk, with his stick.

Then I felt him.

He became my suffering.

He covered me.

I lost consciousness, although my heart did not.

Still my heart called me.

When I awoke from fainting, Bilal was gone.

Hisafa was at my side.

She wiped the blood away.

She gave me medicine and said: take this, it's yours.

And she walked out of my room and into her own.

Hisafa closed her door.

Although I was nine or eight or seven, I was no longer a child.

I was a rag doll.

A doll without voice or will or being in the world.

Red Anemones

I have no country:

Only a part here and a part there—

Under occupation or blockade.

Giving my life to help win back our land: Would that be noble? Would that be heroic?

Would that make something of my worthless existence?

I am a teenager who can think only about sex. What good to have such thoughts as a Muslim child? As a Muslim boy who wants to be good?

I am a son who is ashamed and terrified of his father, an alcoholic, a child beater and a wife beater. Abba has fun-loving moments, but he is weak and ruled by liquor. My mother is ill. I try to care for her. I even want to, although she is usually mean to me. She prefers the attentions of my two younger brothers. I don't know why. Maybe she is embarrassed that I have a stutter that won't go away. It would be like her to feel responsible for having caused it. The way they treat me, both my mom and my dad, may well have been the cause of my stammering.

After we learned to read, one by one, my two brothers and I stopped going to school. All three of us go out and beg day and night in order to keep the household going. We simply cannot find jobs.

In kindergarten I was in a play where we killed our enemies, the Jews. I was praised for performing well, I remember. It is one of the few times I have ever been praised for anything. In a funny way, it may have given me a taste for murder or at least for violence. I have never been fierce looking. Even today they make fun of me, not just because of the way I talk, but because of my smallness. "You are sixteen, your brothers are ten and twelve. Why do you look like you are only eight?"

Every day, someone makes me feel my soft appearance, like a cancer.

Scripture tells me that if I die for a holy cause, if I murder the infidel, the non Muslim, as an act of suicide, then I will be a martyr, a *shaheed*. I will be a tool of *jihad* (holy war), and I will go to Paradise. I will not have to face any of the terrors of the grave, nor will any of my family. Suicide is normally a bad thing for Muslims, but to die in a holy cause, however it is done, makes it blessed. I will no longer be worthless. People will see me for the real man that I am. They will regard me as a hero.

Blessed is a heart that does not stop because of a bullet.

Mahmoud Darwis, poet of Palestine, believed it important to embrace this life, not die for another, but I find inspiration in his beautiful line all the same.

As a suicide bomber, according to my holy readings—scripture and tradition—I will be rewarded by seventy-two *houris* for giving my life. The virgins will have luscious vaginas and pear-shaped breasts; they will not defecate or menstruate or bear children or ever grow old.

What is forbidden in this world will be allowed in the next. Those here in Gaza who encourage me to join Hamas and become a bomber talk about this two-world standard all the time.

Because of my miserable position here on earth, I have decided it is my destiny to become a *shaheed*.

I will miss the red anemones on the hillsides of Palestine.

I will also miss the beautiful horses that I rode in primary school. I can feel the lovely animals cantering beneath me even now.

There is one member of my family whom I truly love, too—my grandfather, Omar, a Muslim in East Jerusalem. I see him only once in a while, whenever I get a rare children's exit pass to travel from Gaza to East Jerusalem for medical reasons. Omar is always good to me. We laugh whenever we are together. No matter how bad I am feeling, my grandfather knows how to make me happy. And can you believe it, he is a stutterer, too!

The suicide bomb will be like a pinch, the terrorists tell me, and then comes rhapsody!

"Just a pinch?" I ask now as I contemplate leaving this, my only world.

I keep chanting the line from Darwis's poem. But I also wonder why the poet himself did not long for the seventy-two virgins of Paradise, as I do. Why did he love this world more than the next?

Blessed is a heart that does not stop because of a bullet.

Because of a bullet or a bomb.

And blessed is Paradise that I may leave Palestine in its bits and its pieces behind me. Then Allah will be my resting place.

Is Allah not my God?

Sambisa

As I fell asleep, I called to my mother. I held her black hand at midnight. I saw her eyes appear in the darkness. I touched her heart in silence.

A forest of many trees, thick with evil, surrounded me as I slept, as I dreamed of early childhood.

Then I awoke. My husband took me again in the night. He spoke no words of love. He grunted sounds of pleasure. Until sleep quieted him once more.

Before my marriage to this man, I had been starved in Sambisa. Starved until I no longer cared about my village, Chibok, or my friends or the air I breathed or the sun when it came. My belly tyrannized me. Only grass was offered me. Grass and starvation for sauce.

Then I united with this soldier of Boko Haram. He chose me at fourteen and made me his slave.

Then full plates of rice and meat replaced outrageous green.

Yes, then they fed me, a Christian girl turned "Islamic" by threat. Freedom had danced away as they whipped me with a *koboko*. I had been studying in Chibok with 275 other girls, ages thirteen to seventeen, for secondary school exams. They kidnapped us on that day, April 14, took us by truck to Sambisa Forest, once cherished by tourists, lovers of foreign animals, but now the camp of another kind of beast, a human one. Would my homeland, would Nigeria, would the government military, save me at last? Could I dare to think so?

Was my papa still alive? Or had he been slaughtered like a pig, as others had, when he returned to Chibok from his timely visit with my uncle?

I was no longer Rifkatu. I was Zainab. Different religion, different name.

A terrorist group with a religion of their own, not true Islam as I had known it through my good friend, Fatia. These were soldiers of jihad, men engaged in a "holy war" against all things Western, all things infidel. "Western education is forbidden." That is what "Boko Haram" means.

During our early years in Chibok, Amina and I were as close as one leaf to another on a single branch. Then she fell in love—here in the forest. Her man was also a jihadist soldier. But unlike my husband, he loved his wife, gave her jewels and pretty dresses, praised her beauty. Brainwashed her so she would betray her best friend.

She and I were alone together one day. Alone in Sambisa Forest. When Aisha—her new name from "Islam"—said to me, "*Allahu Akbar!*" ("God is most great!"), I said in reply, "Our Father who art in Heaven, hallowed be thy name…"

These militant animals of the woods targeted us to be servants of Allah, their own Allah, god of war and death. I would not serve him. Not in my heart. I had thought I could trust Aisha, but she told someone close to her of our conversation. Her action was like a curse disguised as a friend who choked to the point of annihilation.

My husband called me a traitor. He learned through Aisha's husband what I had said. He whipped me until I bled and bled like a butchered dog. I passed out from torment.

There were no secrets in Sambisa. Delicious secrets like my friend and I used to share during our golden years in Chibok. Years with our families and Western learning, my gorgeous star, source of all my dreams.

After I recovered from the whipping, I was permitted to go back to my life of servitude to a man I did not love. The washing, the cleaning, the cooking, the sewing, the being ready for sex at any time. No education—no more hopes of university—only a life of ignorance and slavery.

We did study one book, the Quran, sometimes into the night. I had seen some girls so convinced of the truth of the religion they were being taught, that they were happy when they were chosen to be suicide bombers. In return for their lives, they believed they would gain Heaven immediately and be in the presence of Allah ever after.

Three years after we entered the forest of fanaticism, betrayal, and brutality, government soldiers, the soldiers of Nigeria, came to free us.

It was 2017.

I and 100 others were liberated in that year. But I carried new life within me. I knew that once I arrived back in Chibok, I would be scorned for having been intimate with a terrorist. I had been defiled for carrying his offspring, for having allowed him to enter me. Honor had been violated—I was foul now, according to the belief of my culture. The worst of it was, I physically felt my own shame. I knew that even my papa, if he was still alive, would view me as polluted. You see, he was a very honorable man.

Although Sambisa no longer shrouded me, although I was still alive, unlike my mother and my brothers who had been killed by Boko Haram the day of the kidnapping, still the forest loomed like a power of darkness over me. I never escaped its horror. If, for my pregnancy, I was treated too outrageously by my neighbors and whatever remained of my family, I could always return to the forest, offer my life as a suicide bomber and be done.

Despite my glad moment of liberation, Sambisa had changed my life forever.

Sambisa was like a demon, something stronger than I would ever be.

Toy Shop

At least our baby survived—three operations over two years brought her midsection together again. Mostly, anyway.

Her ten-year-old brother shot her when she was five.

He took a rifle from our open gun rack—there were two other weapons just like it resting there, loaded but harmless. Dad and I told our two kids time and again—you leave those guns alone until you're eighteen. Guns are for adults. They're not for children. They're not toys.

Three rifles, loaded but harmless, resting. Just resting in our small front room.

The doctor of my five-year-old, at St. Louis Children's Hospital, said to me, "You need to lock the guns up so your kids cannot reach them. They're too young to choose to stay away on their own."

"Are you insulting our kids?" I say. They as smart as anyone else's kids. Our whole neighborhood (ask the people next door—either side) has open gun racks, too, or at least guns easy to get to in the house. It's the kind of world we live in down here. Somebody comes in to shoot us—and we're ready for them. Nothing wrong with having our guns ready. Just last month Mrs. Brown down the street shot a child molester—his picture was all over town. It's because she had a gun in easy reach. Otherwise, one or more of her five beautiful children could have been raped or worse.

We take advantage of the law that says you can help yourself to guns, as long as you pay good money.

We may not be able to pay for much else besides clothing and shelter and food, but we do what we need to do to feel safe.

In a neighborhood where there is violence around every corner, our guns give us security. As only guns can.

There they are—three rifles, loaded but harmless, resting. Just resting. In our small front room.

If anyone was at fault for my baby's injury, it wasn't her or her brother, it was Dad and me. We need to drill our kids better on what is a toy and what is not.

But the guns are staying. And they not getting locked up. There ain't no law what says we have to lock them up. In fact, our state say we can carry them right out of the house in the open if we want to. Inside, we need them right at the ready. A gang member, a child rapist, a black-hating policeman can come to the door. We won't be their victim.

I was thinking in church this week, my baby almost died at the hands of her own brother, but then I looked up at the cross: what she did was she almost died on the altar of hope, beneath the cross of Jesus, symbol of what the Bible calls "refuge." Ain't there glory in that? That's what a gun symbolizes for us black folk, in our neighborhood anyway—refuge, a safe place to be—that's how our guns make us feel—like we're safe.

In the hands of the Lord.

Three rifles. Loaded but harmless, resting. Just resting in our small front room.

Voiceless Love

"Why don't you date, Sally!? You're old enough. You're sixteen now!"

These words keep ringing in my ears. They just won't go away. Dad isn't as bad as Mom. "Let her take her time," he says whenever Mom starts getting on me.

I don't think I even like boys. Not yet anyway. All my friends do. In fact, that's all they talk about. Why can't they have my mom for a mom? That would make me happy. I just want to be left alone.

I saw Marie again today. She is so beautiful. She doesn't notice me, of course. She probably never will. I am too plain for anyone to notice. Too gangly and my hair is a mousy brown. She has gorgeous blonde hair and green eyes. Every time she passes me in the hall at school, I just stop and watch her. Her skin is radiant, and she is as slender as a model—not gaunt like an aging bird, like I am. She is as graceful as the swans I see swimming in the Snake River near my home here in Idaho Falls.

Once in the locker room I saw Marie in her underwear. Just looking at her made me feel warm and fuzzy inside, especially down below. There was something different here. I was alarmed. This was not just emotional but sexual attraction, too.

I told my little sister, who's in junior high, about Marie. All I told her was how beautiful Marie is. Even that turned out to be a mistake. "Mom! Sally has a crush on a girl! It's disgusting," I heard her say when she was in the kitchen doing dishes. My mom replied, "I had a crush on a girl once, too, when I was in high school. It will pass. It passed for me. Nothing to worry about. I just wish she'd start dating."

It looks like Marie is going to have to be my secret. I was beginning to be afraid that whomever I confided in would betray me, as Susie had.

About a week after my attempt to talk to my sister, I went to a girlfriend's house after school. It was a Friday. She was giving a buffet dinner for friends, both girls and boys. There was to be dancing. My mom tried to make me go. But I knew Marie would be there, so I went without protest.

As it turned out, Marie was with a guy. She was with the same guy for quite some time. After three or four slow dances together, they began making out.

I felt such jealousy! But there was nothing I could do. It was painful, cruelly painful, for me to watch them. I felt like the little bird in the Thomas Hardy poem we had read in English that week—the bird in "blast-beruffled plume"— only unlike the bird, there was no way I could sing my hope into the barren night. Because I had no hope. No hope at all.

There was something worse, though. I began to think about it seriously for the first time. You see, Marie wasn't my only crush, as Mom, in her Mormon way, had assumed. Marie was just my latest. I had had crushes on women teachers throughout my schooling—and even now: there is Mrs. Bates the young art teacher who seems to like me. She tells me I have talent. My heart beats really fast whenever I am around her. It was the same with teachers in grade school. I loved the pretty ones, the ones who spoke to my heart when they read a poem aloud to the class, or women who made me see a drawing or a painting like I had never seen it before, or teachers who led us all in song in a way that roused me to fervor.

In junior high there was that girl in the playground who sparkled—wasn't it just for me? She was there for me to admire every day during recess. Her name was Loretta. I still remember her petiteness and her glorious red hair.

I began to think, *I have never had these feelings about boys or men.* In a detached way, I have admired the looks of handsome men like President John Kennedy and understood the attraction of a singer like Elvis Presley. But they never touched me emotionally. They certainly have not made me feel sexually aroused, not like Marie was beginning to do. All the earlier women and girls would probably make me feel that way now, now that I am past puberty. I can't help it. It's who I am. I don't see any potential for love with a guy. Not for me. This is not to say I won't marry one someday. I will probably be too weak not to follow the crowd in the end. Why else would I be so afraid that my secret will get out?

Even Dad would start getting on me if he knew my feelings for females. He and Mom are both so religious. Their love for me only goes so far. Their religion comes first. In everything. It makes me feel alone, alone and voiceless—I have never met anyone who is like me. Surely, they must be out there. Why would the church keep coming down on gay people so hard otherwise? All my friends are daughters and sons of church people. As far as I know, they're just like their parents.

I told the friend who had invited me to the party that I wasn't feeling well. I also told her not to call my mother. "The fresh air will do me good," I said.

There was a shorter path, but I deliberately took the long way home.

And so I began the five-mile walk, epiphany pecking like a crow at my heart.

Why Have You Abandoned Me?

"It's August 8!"

"We will meet them today!"

"The agency was disgustingly slow."

"The Smiths warned us."

"What difference does that make? That hasn't helped."

"At least we've had Troy to take care of—for two years now. I feel ready to take on two small children. Besides, the kids will love our dog, just like we do. Love, love! That's all they need."

"Love and faith. If what the agency tells us is true, they have both been treated brutally."

"We will heal their wounds. I know we will. I've been praying for God's help every night."

There was a knock at the door.

Mother, Father, why have you abandoned me?

"Jenny, you get the door. I'll bring out the toys!"

"Okay, Gerald."

The social worker, though usually stern, tried to be friendly—she was eking out what looked like a smile.

"Here are your two children, Beth and Brian. They are seven and nine, brother and sister. They each have sacks from the group home with clothes and underwear in them. We down at the agency hope everything goes well this first weekend. We'll be back to pick them up on Monday morning, early. If all goes well, we'll bring them for a week the next time and if it continues to go well, a check will come at the beginning of every month for as long as they live with you."

Before we could ask any questions or say thank you, she was out the door.

"Are you hungry?" Jenny asked the children. "I've put out peanut butter and jelly and tuna sandwiches for you."

The older child said, looking at a corner of the ceiling, "When do my brother and I get to see our parents again?"

"It's better for you here. We'll be good to you. Look at all these toys! They're brand new. We can play with them after lunch," Gerald said.

"There won't be more children? You'll pay attention to us, right? And you won't drink alcohol, will you, and beat us afterward?" They showed us bruises and welts on their backs.

"This is a sober Christian home," Gerald said. "We'll go to church tomorrow. It's Sunday, the Day of the Lord. And there isn't a bottle or a can of liquor in the whole house. Nor will there ever be."

Both children began to relax.

"Can I have a tuna sandwich?"

"A peanut butter and jelly for me?"

"Of course, sit down. Here is some milk. And fruit salad, too, if you want it."

Suddenly there was loud barking.

"A dog!"

"That's right—he's in our bedroom right now. We'll play with him when we go outside later."

After lunch they had a good game of Monopoly. Then Brian played with toy soldiers and Beth had fun with a new dollhouse. Both of them seemed delighted with their toys for quite some time.

Then Troy was let out. The kids went wild! It was great to hear them laugh and see the flush in their cheeks as they ran around the backyard playing hide-and-go-seek, and tag, with Troy.

They both said they'd never had such a good time. Gerald and Jenny hugged the two kids and each other.

"Okay," Jenny said. She saw that they had been getting tired. "Let's go in for a light supper."

After their meal and cleanup—they saw that the children pitched in with both—the adults showed Beth and Brian their bedroom.

There were no pajamas in their trash bags. Just the sight of the trash bags made Jenny want to cry.

"We always sleep in our underwear," they said.

"It's okay for now. You'll have pajamas and new clothes, too, next time."

Mother, Father, why have you abandoned me?

"When do we get to see our mom and dad? You know, they are getting fixed, so they won't hurt us anymore. It's been two years. They're supposed to be out in three."

"Not this visit," Gerald said. "Next time, though. You'll be here for a whole week so we will have time to arrange something!"

"Now prayers."

"What's prayers?"

"Have you never prayed before?"

"Never heard of it."

"Here is a good one to start. It is called the Our Father. We'll say it again at Church tomorrow!"

Our Father who art in Heaven,

Hallowed be thy name.

Thy kingdom come.

Thy will be done.

On earth as it is in Heaven...

The two children looked at each other. Beth said, "That's pretty, but I don't understand it."

"You don't have to right away. We'll explain a little of it every night."

As they were all walking home from church the next day, Jenny said to the little ones, "Did you understand the Our Father a tiny bit better today?"

"It was boring," Brian said.

"I thought so, too," added Beth.

Jenny was shocked.

Mother, Father, why have you abandoned me?

"Who is this Father?" Brian asked. "Our Father isn't in Heaven, or whatever the word was, he is in an institution for alcohol and I'm waiting to get him back. He was so nice when he wasn't drinking. He gave me a stuffed animal before he left. I would show it to you, but it got stolen at the group home we just came from."

Beth said, "Our mom was the same when she was sober. Why isn't she even mentioned in the prayer?"

Gerald asked, "Did she give you a stuffed animal, too, before she left?"

"She played the piano," Beth answered. "She even gave me a lesson from time to time. My gift was a music box that played Mom's and my favorite song, 'Somewhere over the Rainbow.' One of the teenage foster children at the home took it from me. Otherwise, I'd love to show it to you." Her eyes welled with tears.

Later that night when the kids were asleep, Jenny said to her husband, "They seem so attached to their biological parents!"

"It's going to be hard," Gerald said. "They told us in the classes it would be hard. We need to expect to have to return them to their real parents. But an addiction is very hard to overcome. The whole thing is so unpredictable. It takes strong people to do what we are doing."

"I didn't know how weak I am," Jenny whispered. "In fact, I don't know if I can do it. It's the uncertainty that bothers me most. For some reason I never thought about that before. I guess I figured God would work things out for us. Now that we have met the children, I don't think I can bear it. I love them already, don't you? And at times we seem to be doing them so much good."

"Well," said Gerald, "if we can't do it we can always return them. That's the worst part of fostering: you can't count on their love, but they have to be able to count on yours."

"Maybe we should go the next step on our infertility treatments," Jenny replied. "I think I'm willing to undergo them now, although everyone says they are terrifically painful. Maybe this weekend was God's way of saying He wants us to have our own biological children, no matter what the cost."

"The pain," Gerald agreed. "That was why we stopped, wasn't it? You know the problem could be mine and not yours."

"That was what I thought...but I was afraid to say anything."

"Okay, darling," Gerald murmured. "Let's think about it. Good night."

They kissed and hugged before falling asleep in one another's arms.

Mother, Father, why have you abandoned me?

Wildfire

Wildfire binds the house:

No ordinary flame in

Ordinary time.

Wildfire burns the heart.

Mama cannot speak.

Is it Mama? Or a likeness?

This one who weeps in silence?

She opens the front door

Nods toward school

Holds out, one by one, three brown bags.

Then she embraces one, two, three.

She makes the sign of the cross where the fourth used to be.

Mama weeps silently while others speak.

Nine months now her six-year-old is gone.

Her only girl.

They took the child, the jewel of the house, while she played in the cornfield in the morning sun.

They left a note behind—money or Marie—

That's all it said, one note every month for eight months. "Money or Marie."

We did not have the millions for her sweet arms or legs to return to us.

The reports of Mama's inheritance had been wildly exaggerated.

After eight months, the notes stopped altogether.

Police say Marie…

Police say…

Police…

One month after the notes disappeared

Papa's bloated body was found in the river

On the border of Arkansas.

Papa drank himself to death

As he floated down Ol' Man River.

He loved his liquor.

He never harmed anyone in his drink.

But his stupor always made him seem without life.

Only Marie could make him laugh or dance or sing.

Only his little girl.

Without Marie, there was no joy.

Mama no longer hoped.

Police say Marie…

Police say…

Police…

Mama weeps.

She leaves the words to us boys.

We learned to make our own words

And our own ways in the world.

Our family never was again what it was

When Marie and her yellow dresses,

The polka dot ribbons tied around her braids,

Her little girl's laughter,

Filled our home.

When Marie was alive,

Papa danced.

And Mama looked us boys right in the eye

And called us each by name.

But then the cornfield,

Where the little girl played,

Flared up.

Now it blazes, scorches.

Orange fire, wildfire…

On and on…

Trail of Urine

That little trail of urine—when I threatened to take him back to that place—little dots of yellow that came out as he went up the stairs at home—the memory tugs at my heart, my mother's heart.

But only at mine. His brothers and sisters detest him. Even his own father. His father betrayed him by taking him to the freak house. And he knew it.

I also abhor him much of the time: that monster, that Neanderthal who makes demands I didn't know a child could make. Through him I learned what motherhood is. He made me tolerate for the first time his disabled cousin—the Downs syndrome girl who is, after all, lovable. I no longer feel contemptuous of her or her mother, my sister, as I used to do.

There are moments when I am his mother, only I, I brought him back from that place where everyone else in the family—everyone—wanted him to go. Once I found the address and got there, I had no explanation for wanting the horror back. I only said, "I am his mother."

He, my fifth child, taught me about the world, about being a parent, about being that ugly that tortuous that disgusting that behemoth thing, the thing that people judge you and hate you and feel contempt for you for—the thing they call "mother."

After I brought the small boy back from the debris of the children's bin, I watched my house, my home, crack open like broken glass.

The boy's father, his brothers and sisters, his grandmother, his aunts and uncles hated the animal and so they grew to hate me, the mother of the beast.

Sometimes from out of a life of ugliness and malice he would say about himself, "Poor Ben."

And my heart would move—his father's would not nor his siblings' nor anyone else's—not anyone's—only mine.

I was his mother.

As he grew, his capacity for harm grew—as a small child he had bent back his brother's arm, he killed the dog, then the cat. As he grew, he mauled a child at school. A teenager, he now hangs with a gang that delights in lawlessness, in violence—on television and also in the real world.

I had saved him—I would not let them murder him—that's what they were doing—killing him—slowly at the institution where his father had taken him and where I found him and said to the personnel, "I am his mother."

Once Ben and I had returned home from that place, his four older brothers and sisters began to disappear to aunts' and uncles' houses in the summer and then, as they grew, also during the year. His father kept taking on work so we could keep the large Victorian house we had bought with my father-in-law's money: we had bought it so our large family could dwell in happiness.

And beauty did reign. It reigned over all. Until he came.

Now Ben is gone. He is old enough.

He is sexual now. He has joined a real gang, a gang that robs to support itself and will stop at nothing to get what it wants.

Ben is subhuman—harmful, horrifying—he fits in with the display of raw impulse on which the gang thrives.

I brought him into the world. I raised him and then I let him go—I would not let him be murdered—at that institution—I would not let him be killed— meanwhile I scared away my normal children, all four of them, who are more attached to aunts and uncles than they are to me.

I am their mother, too. But I don't feel it. I belong to Ben and Ben belongs to me. We lived and still live in the same hell, he and I.

Yes.

Ben has taught me what the words really mean, "I am Mother."

Classic Stories of Adults and Children

Abraham

Abraham arose into darkness. The blackness captivated him. He saw stirring before him, small and innocent, Isaac, smiling and blithe and bound by thorns—Isaac, alert, without knowing.

Abraham set his son on the mule. He saw his son but did not look at him. The father's eyes, captivated by darkness, looked toward Mount Moriah and gazed ahead into a long and black tunnel, a tube of awe and terror.

Abraham strode into darkness, speaking aloud but silently as his son lay sleeping, nodding to the pace of the steadily moving mule toward the sacrifice.

The son of Abraham dismounted the mule at the top of Moriah, at the foot of crossed wood, at the base of the blood and the father.

Abraham reached into the darkness that captivated him. The darkness of Mount Moriah. He sought and found tools for his deed. His holy deed. He found blood and nails in the heart of the darkness that seized him.

The father took his tools and nailed his son until he bled. His beloved son, the long-awaited son of his age.

The father, enamored of darkness heard as holy word, directed himself to a funeral pyre where he burned Isaac after torturing him with blood and nails.

The father tortured and killed his only son on behalf of One no words can describe, for a reason words cannot capture, for a love and a trust beyond the understanding of brothers and sisters in mourning for a crucified divinity who dwells everlastingly beyond the face of the world.

Ceres

I sat outside in the rain.

I waited for the sun.

Then I felt moisture again.

I watched the moonlight come and go.

For nine days and nights I did not move.

Like an oppressive stone or the frigidity of prison walls, grief tormented me.

An old man and his daughter walked by me.

"Be happy in your daughter," I said. "I have lost mine."

And we wept together for the breaking of the treasure that bound us.

As I continued the search, crossing many lands, lead centered my heart.

Then, back in Sicily, the fountain Arethusa told me a secret. She had seen Proserpine—my daughter had become queen of the underworld, stolen by the enamored King Pluto.

I went to Pluto's brother in the skies, the almighty Jupiter.

The Fates forbid the eating of any food in the dark world if one wants to return to the light of day. It seems my child had eaten the juice of a pomegranate. And so she could never return to earth.

When I heard this, I could not accept it. I, goddess of the harvest, struck a bargain with Jupiter. Every winter, my heart will need mending, even as the earth will become barren. Proserpine will be as absent to me then as a dead man, for she will dwell with her husband in Hades. But every spring the earth will bloom again, and my daughter will ascend from the underworld. Her touch, for a time, will heal and resurrect a buried heart.

Child and Father: Battleground

Is this what is really real? This monster, this freak, this invading army?

How could I ever have compared the aberrant baby to a wounded soldier, a human being injured on the dark battlefields of World War I? How could the sight of him have invoked the injured Apollinaire?

How could I have wept for the little one's misery when he is the source of mine?

A baby with two heads, my baby—is it not he who is invading my quiet field?

Will I enter forever a nightmare world for his sake?

Or will I see to it that the freak is murdered so I may live?

I needed a bottle of whiskey the day of the news, as I had never needed one before. I puked my much-needed hangover all over my classroom floor.
The result: I have no job.

I will divorce my wife—mother of the disaster—after I get rid of the child.

Then I will be completely free.

I am still in my twenties—finally I can live my dream. I can show what I am made of by exploring the wilds of Africa, at last! Dreams of this adventure I have nursed for years. But why does the thought of liberation not inspirit me? My somberness recalls Kikuhiko. Why can I not forget him? He owns a gay bar now. He has called it after himself. He is choosing to commit himself to his sexual orientation. He is not running from anything. He is completely, personally free. Why was he contemptuous of me when we last spoke—just as I used to be disgusted by him years ago? Unlike Kikuhiko, why do I feel like a man who is running? Running as fast as I can? Running from a baby I will kill and a wife I will divorce?

If I run from the baby, the freak with the brain hernia, do I not run from myself?

What was it my wife said to me in the hospital maternity ward: Are you the kind of man who abandons the weakest? As you abandoned Kikuhiko long ago, when he needed you most?

Am I that kind of man? Am I the craven foot soldier, the coward who turns and runs?

Himiko gave me great sex when I was facing the pit of nightmare fatherhood. And she wants to share the adventure of Africa with me. She has a friend, an abortionist, who does forbidden things.

But Himiko cannot give me what I need most.

No one can—I need the courage to be.

Valor is something that running away does not require.

Only one thing does demand forbearance: standing in place with the rest of the suffering world—standing, quiet as a murdered child, in the army of humankind.

Children's Game

Doc says my delivery might not go well. I told him my baby had stopped moving. So here I am in the hospital—waiting.

Wrote to "Dad" about sending me money. Didn't know who else to write to, Mom being dead and all. I still think "Dad" killed her, although he swears he didn't.

Dad's been my dad for about five years. He met my mom and me when I was twelve.

Humbert Humbert—that's the weird name he called himself when he wasn't playing with me or fondling me or fucking me.

I had nowhere else to go—but with him—once Mom died. So "Dad" and I went on a road trip together. Motel after motel, bed after bed, fuck after fuck.

When I was twelve Humbert led me to believe I was right, that sex was a children's game and he didn't know how to play it, that he never had played it as a child. This guy at school and I used to fuck behind the bushes—so I thought I knew more than Humbert did. I taught him. For fun.

I learned different afterward. His organ ripped me open hour after hour, day after day, night after night. He had known, all right. He had known all about it. What he didn't know was that I couldn't help weeping every night after he was asleep. I wept like a baby, like a little child, the one I was or used to be.

Finally, after insisting on keeping me to himself, he let me out into the world. He let me go to a girl's school. That was when I met Clare Quilty. He was a famous playwright. A crush felt good after two years of loathing with a guy who killed my mom just so he could be with me day in and day out, just so he could fuck away what was left of the child inside me.

But Clare didn't want me, it turned out. What Clare wanted was for me to be in his porno movie. Once I found out, I said *no*.

Of course, Humbert broke me—broke my life.

Clare broke my heart.

Then after a while I found Dick. I liked Dick and he wanted to marry me. I was seventeen by then. I got pregnant and here I am.

Dad's money helped us—he gave me four thousand dollars when he stopped by after he got my letter asking for four hundred. Humbert looked real strange. Once he knew why I left him, I could tell that he was going to go after Quilty. Anyway, he listened while I explained.

Then…Humbert asked me to come back with him. I remember what I said in reply. I said, "No, honey, no."

He must have killed Quilty by now, given his intensity about me and what he called his Annabel Lee complex—the young girl from Edgar Allan Poe's poem about love and death.

Have you read it?

Don't know if I'll outlast this pregnancy.

What would I do with a child of my own? What would I do with it? How would I raise it?

What does it mean to be a child?

Here come the doctors—one of them has eyes like Humbert—a green-eyed monster with a snake's tongue and a man's frickin' fleshy pistol bulging up from inside his pants.

Here they all come—these old men.

They're going to open my private parts in a different way. They're not going to do it like "Dad" did, but still they'll do it.

Don't know if I'll be able to stand it.

No.

This will be the last time. I can feel it.

The baby doesn't feel like it's going to live either.

If only I had been left alone. When I was a child, a twelve-year-old child, a child by the beautiful sea.

Cordelia

"Delia, Delia…"

He used to call me that.

When I was a little girl, when I was just beginning to walk, to talk.

"Delia, come unto me, my precious maid. Come to me!"

And he would pick me up and kiss me until I could no longer breathe a child's breath.

He kissed me until I cried and laughed, "Stop, Daddy! Stop!" I giggled into my tiny hands and smiled for him—for my father and my king.

I didn't smile once, though, on the day I tumbled into darkness.

Why did he blow out my candle? Was it because he was old by then and he needed me beyond his own heart and words? Needed me like a lamb needs its mother's teat? Was that it?

He took me and he threw me with his own hands into the darkness. Was it because I did not want to play anymore? I was eighteen. I had put away childish things. I was a grown woman seeking a grown man for a mate. That man was not him, not my father, once king of my heart.

There was war in the kingdom after he banished me for not playing his game. His game of words. I would not flatter him like my sisters did. That was all he wanted. He did not want real love, adult love. He did not ask for love at all, even though he said he did.

On that black day, at eighty years old, he gave my inheritance to my dog-hearted sisters, who never played with him in the time of play—never once did they play with him in childhood, but only now, on the day he dangled his kingdom before them. Then they played. They played for the earth, for the dirt beneath my father's feet. It concealed jewels and wealth beyond measure. Then they played. They played and they won.

But I had given up childish things.

"No, Father," I said when my turn came. "I will play no longer."

My sisters and their so-called husbands went to war in daylight after I chose the beautiful hovel of adulthood for my own.

Here we are now, my father. We are together in a prison, our natural home. We play no games here. Prisons and death belong to the old and the captured. Finally, after having been cast into the storm by your two-faced daughters, deep pangs of rejection—your first in a long life—bemadden you.

Now, having come back to the real world, you expect nothing of me. Together we sing a serious and beautiful tune, a sober song with a bewitching adult cadence. A song of love.

We dance together: a transcendent movement of affliction and death. We dance a dance that suffuses the barren earth today with the rich rain of a love that does not dwell in the garden of the child.

We will die soon, you and I, but not without having lived and loved in secret, in a tower together far above the noisy play of the world, a world buckling at the knees.

Like blue-eyed cats, we smile high above the jarring din of the warring world.

Dearheart

Don't love too much

no thing worse

when you have only the empty to love from

Don't love too much

if you do your freedom will drown

bars of jail will conquer you

Don't do it

or haunting will be a problem

spooky times will be your day

terror will live inside you like a split tree

Don't love too much

or you'll kill her

the one you love

so suffering will

pass her by

suffering like you have known

lived with

buried inside you

If you do it

you may die

or she or they all may die

and you live with the dying inside

When they stripped you

when they tied you to a chokecherry tree

when they whipped your back

when they sucked milk from your mama breasts

when they raped you

you learned what slavery means

to be a thing for man without skin

You were Free for a while

But when a schoolteacher came to where you live

when he came to 124

when white man came to take not you

but your children and swallow them—all four

when he came to take their spirits away from you

and away from them

you could not help but love too much

You try to kill them

all with love

to turn them to nothing

nothing does not know agony

nothing does not know violation or humiliation

But only one

only your beloved died

only the little one whose throat you slit

only she died

to live and frighten you

for days on end

Even when you loved her

you knew your love was too thick

you loved too much

you killed too much for love

Then your beloved

appeared to you

she appeared from the grave in the water

Then she loved you

but she haunted you too

like a ghoul

a beautiful ghoul

from the dirt

from the dungeon

from no more

But she stopped her game

her game of touch and taste

her game of snare

She was not your one best thing

she was not

Paul D taught you to let go of behemoth

he taught you to let go of love

to let go

to say goodbye

to accept

that you not she

are your own best thing

And so she freed you from herself

the one you loved more than you loved yourself

Love has limits

even for a used-to-be slave woman

a thing of man without skin

who wishes happiness not terror on her daughter

of a little one who cannot grow

into agony

into a tree

a cross she cannot carry

But no more can mama mama mama

the one who loves too much

You were only trying to outhurt the hurter

but you loved too much

Now you know

she is not your own best thing

but you are

Paul D he loved you

he told you

you your own best thing

you free

from slavehood

But you also free from

the baby what you kill

because you love too much

You twice a slave

once to men without skin

once to a dear darlin you love too much

She finally went back

to the darkness in water whence she come

that means you free, dearheart, you free

You belong now

you belong to you

to only you

that what freedom mean

Love: Dream or Reality?

Have you read in the newspaper how an eight-year-old boy was killed by a pack of hounds? A general let the pack loose on the boy because he had injured the paw of his favorite dog. Of course, the little one was eviscerated, torn apart within minutes.

Or picture a five-year-old girl genuinely hated by her parents—I take all my examples from real life, Alyosha—the girl soiled herself and was put in the outhouse at night in the cold. Her mother smeared the child's face with excrement and then made her eat it. She was sexually aroused by her daughter's defenselessness.

In the army, Turks showed a baby a shiny pistol. The baby laughed without knowing until its brains were blown out. These same Turks carved fetuses from their mother's wombs and tossed newborn babies into the air then caught them on their bayonets, laughing as the newborns squirmed in agony.

Alyosha, my love for innocent children, little ones such as these, makes it impossible for me to accept the world. What was it your elder, Father Zossima, said about love? Love in reality is a harsh and dreadful thing compared to love in dreams. I have been wondering lately, is my love for tortured children only a dream?

I will lose my mind in the end. I know I will let my brother kill my father. One reptile will devour the other. It is the way of things. They will follow the law of nature. They—and you and I—are part of an order where only the strong survive.

I will suffer as I have never suffered before when Father is killed—not by Dmitri, as we all suspect, but by Smerdyakov, our half-brother, who believes as I do, who learned from me and will act on what he has learned—there is no good and evil: there is only strong and weak. And only the strong survive.

Alyosha, don't talk of children as I do. Don't envision only their torment. Don't philosophize from their suffering, even if it is real. Love them as they are, not just in their naivete, but also in their true viciousness, their bullying, their demanding self-centeredness; love the hard way, as I will fail to do because I do not believe in God.

I will suffer and probably die of this battle between my head and my heart: "brain fever" they will call it. Only you, my little priest-to-be and people like you, will suspect that the breach exists where no scalpel can follow.

Filicide I

Iphigenia, your evening songs used to captivate family and guests with their beauty.

Now those lips I gag.

The sacrifice of a virgin is required to allay her wrath—Artemis, goddess of the hunt.

I see you, my cheeks wet with tears, I see you breathing: my daughter's life for the life of the sacred stag I killed.

But you, the glory of my house? Here at Aulis, port of anguish?

The harness of necessity I affix.

Fate has called the Greek army to avenge at Troy the stealing of Helen from her husband, Menelaus. Artemis, pale with anger, withholds the needed winds.

After your murder, still wearing the yoke, I will be driven by gales across the ocean to the killing fields of Troy.

My hated filicide will give me a foretaste of the blood of the young men I slaughter on foreign plains.

When, at last, your father meets you in the underworld, my darling, will you wrap your arms around him?

Will you transfix him with your tears?

Filicide II

No, Mommy! No! Don't kill us!

Why do you do what you do?

You love us! Don't you love as you have said?

I cannot kill them. I bore them. Their bridal beds I will adorn when they take wives, and they will nurse me in age.

Bearing and raising and enjoying children, watching as they mature, lying in their arms in the final moments: this is what it means to live.

But Jason is coming. The king's people are coming to kill both me and my darlings.

Who better to take these lovely young lives but the woman who gave them birth?

My poisoned robe, dazzling the unsuspecting princess, has killed her, Jason's young love. Caressing his only daughter, the king also died of the poison. All this according to plan.

Not for nothing did Jason trade me, his mare, for a young filly.

I know, Corinthian women, I know, you have said it is better not to give birth than to bear and raise children in necessary pain. At every stage of a child's growth there is danger. And *moira*—Death—strikes in the end. Even if I do not butcher my young boys, the toad, the black toad of illness, or the cruel net of years will take them in the end.

And yet I feel sorrow at the silence I will cause. But I can endure being the clown that disguises hatred as laughter. I can endure, because Jason will have to share in my grief at the empty, echoing room. Yes, in the same way, he too will transgress the halls of the innocent dead. Even in his sleep he will walk, guilt-ridden, through the vast kingdom of Hades.

The black, shriveled heart does not revert to green.

Goddamn Savior

I couldn't. I couldn't. I goddamn couldn't. I wanted to save him, to catch him, from the goddamn cliff as he played in the rye. I really did. But I couldn't. So I got mad and smashed the windows in my garage, every one of them, every goddamn window in the goddamn garage. I broke my hand. My mom took me to the hospital. But Allie was dead, no matter what either of us did. Leukemia was a killer, a killer that was hiding, lurking for my younger brother, waiting for him at the edge of the field. This is what all of us, all of us goddamn human beings, have to deal with—the cliff at the edge of things. There is no one there to save us, goddamn no one there to catch us in the rye as we fall fall fall and cannot stop. There is no one there to save us as we play or just live in the goddamn rye.

My mom never got over it. After she unlocked the one window on the inside, she sealed up goddamn Allie's room on the outside. Only she, his only mother, could go inside, she said. Two times a year she'd open his window and climb into the sanctuary—that's what she called it. On his birthday and on the day he died. Every year. I don't know what she did in there on those two days. I really don't. But my dad, Phoebe, and my older brother, DB, we respected her need. We really did. My mom would have gone goddamn berserk if she hadn't had this one tiny thing, this ritual. She really would have and we knew it.

Allie was two years younger than me. I loved him. I loved him like a bastard.

Really ugly girls, my ten-year-old sister Phoebe, because she with her wild red hair and her love of things (it was all natural!)—she is just a goddamn kid—all kids are great, even when they sleep and drool all over the pillow—they look nice, more than stupid adults who snore and sleep with their mouths wide open—

Anyway, really ugly girls, my sister Phoebe, my brother DB's stories before he sold out to Hollywood—they were goddamn masterpieces of the inner heart—very real. I'm not kidding (nothing phony there!). Also the song "Little Shirley Beans" by Bessie Smith, the black woman who knew all about emotion and where it really comes from, from the goddamn guts of the heart (it really does), when I suddenly cry like a bastard, or when I wear my red hunting cap backward, just how I like it (who cares what the goddamn rest of the world thinks?), or totally unlike that jazz pianist Ernie or the famous actors, the goddamn Lunts, who just perform to get applause—unlike those three—the guy who plays the big drum in the orchestra at Radio City—he only gets to sound his drum about two goddamn times in the whole piece but he never looks bored (and it sounds so sweet—it really does)—anyway these are a few (probably the only goddamn ones) of the things that I have goddamn sympathy for and don't hate. These and Jane Gallagher, who never cared if she won or lost at checkers—she just liked seeing them crowned in the back row, so she kept them there. That really knocked me out. (I feel like goddamn vomiting when I think of my roommate at Pencey—Stradlater—who wanted to give old Jane the time in his teacher's car—he wanted to get inside her goddamn pants—he really did—and he didn't even know her. Or care. Just the thought of the handsome creep makes me want to vomit.) People—especially little Phoebe—say I don't like anything, but, you see, I do. Those two nuns I met at the diner who collect money for the poor in their spare time—they really knock me out.

Mostly, though, I'm depressed as a bastard. And I want to die. Because I flunked out of school again—too many goddamn phonies in the school, including the teachers, and too many goddamn phony things you have to do. There or at any school where I'm always supposed to grow up and join the phony adult world.

Even Phoebe just said, "Dad is going to kill you," when I said I flunked out of this last school, Pencey—just like I did at Elkton Hills—and for the same goddamn reasons. I could list a million things that are already listed in this goddamn book that I hate—all the phonies—there are plenty of them. Mostly they are like Mr. Haas, the headmaster at Pencey. He likes a parent if she's stylish and rich, but if she's fat or shabby-looking he just turns the other old way.

I'm goddamn depressed. And I know I need help. When I was watching lil Phoebe on the carousel in Central Park this afternoon, I admitted that the kids—like my red-haired sister—and me, goddamn it—and me—won't always be kids (I mean I'm already sixteen!)—and sometimes I won't be able to catch them—the innocents—in the rye (this is the one job I dream of ever having, whether I finish school or not). I just have to admit—I really do—that they (and, okay, I!) have to grow up, take goddamn risks, like when you reach for the gold ring on the carousel Phoebe's riding: you could fall off or you could actually catch the gold ring. It's just the way life is.

Yep, I am crying right now like a bastard—I have to admit that they have to lead lives—even I do—without a savior like me by the cliff at the edge of the field of rye.

I haven't figured it all out yet.

I have to go to the goddamn hospital before I even try. My nerves are shot. I'm still nearer the goddamn child than the adult. Thank God.

I am trying. I am trying to deal with this goddamn life. This goddamn world.

I really am.

Heaven 'n' Hell

I been asked to dissertate 'bout something: Ain't used to this kind o' truck but I reckon I can do it.

Aunt Polly says she'll give me a whole TEN BUCKS If I don't do no lyin'. SO!

Goin' to bust myself: watch me.

One BUCK per minute. A purty serious subjeck. I ain't used to bein' serious like this but I figure ten bucks is ten bucks.

I told myself I'd go to hell for him. Didn't like the idea of hell and all that Sunday-school truck but I said I'd go there for him. He'd been so good to me—though he was a n****r on the outside, he was a white man on the in. I swear, so maybe there is a hell somewhere that's only hell on the outside and it's heaven on the in. Maybe that's the kind o' hell I'll be goin' to.

'Gardless, even if it be a sin to steal Miss Watson's n****r, I ain't goin' to turn my friend in what takes my long hours of watch in the deep of night so I can sleep, and what loves his fambly just like white folk do. More than white folk do, since my family, all white, is Pap. Pap tol' me once I should steal a chicken whenever I could. If I didn't want it, somebody would. A good deed ain't never forgot, he said, though he never showed me he meant those last words, only the stealin' part.

I can't think of a time he did me any good. He didn't even want me to go to school, ya know, because he ain't never had no learnin' hisself. But mostly it was when he was drunk—he got mighty ornery. That was when I learned what no young'n should have to learn. That was when I learned all about fear, inside and out.

Aunt Sally now, she's white just like Pap but she's got some o' Jim in her. The way she give me a lickin' for fooling her, the whippin' wasn't never worth shucks. Then she stayed up all night crying when Tom disappeared. Aunt Sally did have some o' Jim in her—natural-like. She cared for her kin, even real distant kin like me who ain't really no kin to her at all. She mothered me good and made me feel guilty I ever tricked her like I did with them spoons and other truck Tom and I took from her house to free Jim who was already free. Tom give Jim forty bucks for putting up with all the phony escape antics he put Jim through. Jim who was already free, Tom knew, according to what they call Miss Watson's will.

Jim were happy with the bucks though—didn't hold nothin' against Tom. Not to my knowledge he didn't.

Okay. Here is the most serious part, the part Aunt Polly wanted to hear me talk about. She said I'd be good at it. Imagine that. Nobody never told me nothin' like that before.

Jim and Sally taught me about the good in (I'm going to use a fancy phrase now) human nature.

Pap and the real white king and duke, they teached me about the dark side. Which is everywhere. The good ain't got no color nor no sex nor age neither. The good just be. It shines in what I call the darkness.

Okay.

Was that ten bucks worth it? Whether it was or not, it threw my innards out o' whack. You know why? It didn't have in it a single stretcher!

I, Icarus

I am excited: I have wings.

I turned thirteen this year!

My feathers grow every day.

New feathers sprout: do you see them?

In ten days, I will be free.

Free of Daedalus: my dad.

The flight will liberate us both from this tower where even my father is captive.

He seeks his freedom, I mine.

This is why he crafted wings for us.

I am going to soar above him on the day we leave. I am going to be myself for the very first time. My strong young self.

Now only five days remain. I can feel my muscle!

I am going to seek and I am going to find the golden prize.

I am going to soar upward until I reach the sun.

Dad says to stay near him, not to fly too close to the light of the world.

He's trying to hold me back, to keep me down.

He wants me to think he's the light that shines over all.

My whole miserable childhood I have spent as his slave.

A new light beams inside and tells me so.

No more!

After I've seen the sun up close, the light outside us all, the source of illumination and joy, I will have a story to tell.

I will tell my story to Iphigenia.

When I return from the adventure of diamond light, I will reveal to Iphigenia who I have become. She will gaze and gaze and fall in love with the light I have become.

So runs my faith.

We are nearly ready for the flight. Only one more day now.

"Son, do not fly too near the sun. Your waxen wings will melt and you will fall into the sea."

I have had enough warnings. All from him. He doesn't understand. He won't admit that I am young and he is old or that, yes, I will rise above him!

I am going to do as my own heart, my own joy, my own self dictates.

He will keep me down, he will hold me in a bridle, in his own soft but painful bridle, no more!

Yes! Yes!

I am in the air now!

I flap my wings. My beautiful wings.

I am soaring upward.

I cannot stop.

I will not stop.

Freedom is too wonderful when it seizes your heart and your limbs and propels you toward gold and blue. What human being has ever done this?

No one.

No one but I: I, Icarus!

The sun is gorgeous, as gorgeous as my love, Iphigenia.

The sun is the center, the new center of my world.

The sun is my god. My one true god. I move closer and closer to the golden rays. The glorious sun will claim me for its own.

But what is happening?

My wings feel weak.

I stretch out my arms in worship. But the lovely ball of light is disappearing.

How can that be?

Are my wings melting?

No! No!

"Father!"

He is not there.

Paternal hands and their guiding ways are not within reach.

This is a bad dream. It cannot be real.

Though a dream, I am not waking!

Or is it a dream?

I am not waking.

No: I am plunging toward the sea.

The yellow sun grows smaller and smaller. My wings are impotent.

I am impotent.

Iphigenia flashes before me. I reach for her. I embrace not a body, but a vision: I fondle a mirage.

Death is not freedom.

It was not a story of death I was expecting to tell.

I feel the water in my mouth: the cold wetness covers my eyes and my hair.

It takes my life into its maw and sucks me into blackness.

The light disappears, I descend into the darkness.

Only now do I see the light that guides, the light of Daedalus, the light that radiated as I grew.

A light I could have followed but chose not to. I, Icarus, I made the choice of lights.

I chose the sun.

I longed to be a man.

I, Icarus, I turned thirteen this year…

Does that not mean something?…

A young man yes, but a man with…

Wings and an "I"…to make me fly on wings of awe…

I, Icarus…a man with wings…of boldness…

A boldness…

All…my…own…

Keys to the Kingdom

When my sister took it upon herself to raise me—she abused both me and her husband, Joe.

But Joe's heart was a kingdom. I learned things from Joe that conquered injustice that loomed everywhere else in our house. Joe was afraid of doing to his own wife what his father had done to his mother, so instead of fighting back he just accepted Tickler (the stick my sister used when her temper raged) whenever it struck him. One evening when we were alone: he told me he knew that his own cruel father—an abusive alcoholic—had meant well through all his damaging behavior. Joe was proud of the epitaph he had written for him: "Whatsume'er the failings on his part, remember, reader, he were that good in his heart."

I was a child, but Joe was a child too in the kingdom of the heart.

When I was only six years old the criminal Magwitch terrified me, but I also pitied him. When I brought him food and a file for his chain as he had ordered, I was glad to see that he enjoyed the dinner I lay before him. And I told him so as I watched him gobble his vittles like a starving dog.

It turned out Magwitch never forgot that moment or those words—how I treated him like a human being and not the thug that he was. Later he was sent to Australia after having been tried and found guilty of a crime in England. It was his memory of me as a young boy that kept him going and gave his life purpose. He worked hard in Australia. He wanted me to be what he never could be—he had been an orphan and a hungry one at that—in and out of jail almost since he had been born. Now, he made money so I, a poor blacksmith's boy, could rise in society and become an educated gentleman. I at least could be comfortable and respectable, even if he never had been or could be.

I was a child, but Magwitch was a child too in the kingdom of the heart.

I possessed the keys to the kingdom when I was quite young, but the wealthy Miss Havisham tempted me to release them. She tempted me through her beautiful daughter, Estella. Estella's beauty and wealth made her proud. Miss Havisham was raising the girl to break hearts just as her own heart had been broken when she was abandoned at the altar many years before.

When I met Estella (we were both eight) the child in me left the kingdom of equals and I began to worship the girl. She made me feel for the first time that my hands were coarse, my speech was common, my boots were shabby. I wanted Estella's good opinion. That was the only thing I did want from the day we met. For many, many years I did not change.

Thus, my childhood had brought me both a transcendent kingdom and a worldly enemy of it.

Through a misunderstanding encouraged by Miss Havisham, I thought Estella would be mine one day. I thought that the traumatized mother of Estella was the patron who through the lawyer Jaegers sponsored my rise in society. I had no inkling that the actual sponsor was the criminal whose heart I had touched as a young boy. However, Estella married not me but a wealthy man who turned out to be violent. Estella suffered two years of marriage to him before he died.

My beloved Joe knew that he was beginning to embarrass me as I rose in society, so he stayed out of my way. Appearing cheerful, he avoided me out of respect for my feelings. I knew perfectly well, though, that my behavior wounded him. During that time, I became capable of any meanness toward Joe. I did not yet know that the golden keys I possessed but ignored were keys to a kingdom far beyond anything that belonged to the world.

Though he was sentenced to exile in Australia for life, Magwitch returned to England in order to see how the gentleman he had created was progressing. Of course, once I learned that the escaped Magwitch and not Estella's mother had been my patron, I could no longer live as a gentleman. All my worldly hopes, I finally realized, had been illusory.

After I did what I could to safely return Magwitch to Australia, I returned home to Joe. I told him and his new wife, sweet Biddy: I knew now that over the past years the building I thought I was soon to inhabit was more like a swamp than the palace I had taken it for. In short, until lately I had been living in a land of dreams.

When I looked at Joe that day, I saw that he was offering me again the keys to the kingdom he had given to me as a child.

I took them.

This time I had no intention of giving them up in return for lesser things.

Although as a young man I had been sucked in, the swamp had no more power to lure me away from a kingdom that I had since learned was far above the world.

Love Feast

I had gotten used to it because of my disease. But this one I would remember forever—or at least until the curse had been played out.

My brother seemed to forgive me my affair with his wife and my failed attempt at his throne. At first, he banished me from the kingdom but then—he asked me back. When he opened the front door of the palace, I was struck by his handsome face. I read only love and forgiveness there. Atreus always had been mysterious, but I was beginning to think now that he was good.

Meanwhile I let him send my small children, whom I had brought with me, to one of the servant women. She would feed and care for them as Atreus and I celebrated our reconciliation—which, I suspected, could only have come from on high.

My brother offered me a golden throne for a chair. For some reason this did not surprise me. Then I was served exquisite wine from the royal cellars. After the libations, Atreus himself served me a pie. It was a meat pie, as far as I could tell. I began eating. A real delicacy. I had never tasted anything like it before. But as I continued the feast, I noticed something unseemly. Was it the smell? The touch? The taste?

As I picked at the pieces, I became alarmed. I poked at them, bits of fingers, remnants of toes. I recognized them.

I vomited.

Atreus, appearing the perfect host, revealed himself to be the blackest traitor. Like a human tree struck at the root I, Thyestes, cursed Atreus and his entire house. I cursed his generations. I was like a Fury bent on the wildest revenge.

Once again, I fled my homeland. My one surviving son, Aegisthus, was at my side. Aegisthus had been spared because he was too old, his flesh not tender enough to be cooked, like his brothers, in a pie.

*   *   *

King Agamemnon, son of Atreus, slew his daughter Iphigenia;

Queen Clytemnestra, wife of Agamemnon, son of Atreus, slew Agamemnon for his slaughter of their daughter;

Aegisthus, son of Thyestes, and lover of Clytemnestra, took part in Agamemnon's slaying;

Orestes, son of Agamemnon, slew Clytemnestra and his uncle, Aegisthus, for their killing of his father.

*   *   *

So ended the curse uttered by Thyestes against Atreus and his generations—a curse pronounced because through beguilement Atreus had tasted the limbs of his own children served to him in a pie.

Niobe

Gone.

My one joy.

One.

Gone.

One-in-fourteen as if the one had never been.

My joy turned to grief when my best friend told her children—there were two of them—to kill my children: seven boys and seven girls—radiant, beautiful.

They said it was because I had bragged. I bragged that I had fourteen children and she had only two.

So what if her two were mighty gods of Olympus? My children, just like all children, are like Olympians to the woman who suffers the agony of childbirth, the arrow of motherhood.

I suffered the arrow fourteen times, she only twice.

Had I not the right to brag of my suffering? Had I not the right to tear joy from the womb of sorrow?

Pride, they said, brings bad things.

I should have walked humbly before Latona and her two divine ones.

Artemis killed my seven girls with her poisoned arrows.

Apollo killed my seven boys with his.

Neither they nor their mother, Latona, understood the sacredness of the bond between mother and child.

All three were hard-hearted in their ignorance: they were murderers without knowing.

I could only weep when I saw the bodies. I could only weep as I watched them fall one by one.

I melted as I witnessed the poisoned arrows: boulders racing toward a finish line.

Now that's all I can do. I have turned to stone.

But my heart is not hard.

My heart still weeps.

I have congealed into rock, but my maternal heart is soft as water.

My heart weeps and my heart gushes sorrow for the grief of all mothers whose suffering is not seen, whose love is not worshipped as divine.

Paint My Face

Let them call me insane, let them call me subhuman, let them call me a mad dog.

I killed his two sons after I blinded Polymestor. Who can describe the torture of a parent bereaved? And what parent has been as bereaved as I? All my sons but one, lost in war, and that one, my youngest love, Polydoros, slain by Polymestor, friend turned traitor.

Offspring for offspring: the only way of showing Polymestor what real grief is.

After Troy had fallen, my daughter Polyxena, my sole companion in captivity, was sacrificed in front of the Greek army. My brave soldier, without a killing field, freely offered her whiteness to the darkness of the enemy. My royal one: doll, figurine, toy embellishment for Achilles' tomb.

And Hades will take Cassandra, my last daughter, sex slave of Agamemnon, by the vigilant hand of Clytemnestra, wife of her bed's companion. This they prophesy.

Draw a picture of my face and you will draw the shadow of a dead woman, the profile of one who has lost nineteen children: all her pretty ones.

For my two murders and my blinding, let them call me insane, let them call me subhuman, let them call me a mad dog.

Pieta

I faced the impenetrable every day.

Now it is over.

Today mystery in your eyes floods my heart, even as it cleanses the sullied treasures of the earth.

As an adolescent you startled. You separated.

But today I wear your crown of thorns: it is my own.

The scourges, the metal entering your hands and feet bloody my clothes, pierce my own arms and legs.

I weep for your living body.

Your birth, your cry across the abyss.

I have come home this hour.

Home to the light born of darkness, home to the boon born of hammer and sword.

I love the beating heart that beats no more.

I love the salt water I empty,

The liquid you shed,

The pulse of the tomb,

The key to all that bears mystery or joy.

Rosebud, my glory and my shame,

Forever my secret heart beats a koan: our enigma.

My criminal, my God, my climbing and descending vine, my little one grown big with suffering, my man grown small with bruises from the black reservoir where your tender agony forever echoes across the barrenness, a new beauty of the earth.

Prodigal

I, ghostlike on the porch, walk forth and back again staring blue-eyed outward then upward toward the night sky.

I ascend stairs to a roof window: I look far, and I look near: I want to honor my eyes with her hair.

My heart in my hand, elder daughter at my side, I pocket strange love for the day.

Tomorrow my absent one will pull once more as I search for emblems, for traces she still lives, for signs she still has being in the world.

Maybe tomorrow she will appear covered in pig's slop quaking with fear.

She will come empty-handed but full-mouthed with a smile—with the sparkling smile of humility she will dazzle me.

Or do I dream?

Maybe tomorrow I will embrace her finger. Bejewel it with a bright red gem.

Maybe tomorrow, elder daughter by my side, your sister will speak within hearing; she will speak our tongue and our words in our world.

She, a party girl, asked, and I gave her her inheritance to enjoy young. So I placed before her a forked road. She thus began the journey perilous.

By now her hippie's garb is torn and dirtied by the slop of the swine she has embraced during long lonely nights of destitution.

Is it only a dream?

Do I dream that she will return and that you, gentle one, will envy her, will envy her then?

I warn you now. I will throw a celebration like none known to woman or man.

I warn you now.

I will call

    the butcher

    the pastry shop

    the purveyor in happy wine

all will gladden the heart.

Don't complain, darling, as I know you will, don't complain that your prodigal sister has returned to a house of celebration, not a prison of judgment.

I will say to you on that day, the day of our glory, "You are always with me. But this your sister was dead and is alive again. She was lost and is found."

Or my good, my loyal one, am I dreaming?

Will your little sister never return, return for the festivity I already prepare in my mind for a young child now grown, for a wandering adolescent trailing a golden star, for the young adult who seeks now a better somewhere to find?

AM I DREAMING, Esther?

Or is it her hair that I glimpse?

Is it my heart that beats as it has never beat before?

Call

    the pastry shop

    the butcher

    the purveyor in happy wine

I hold the jewel in my hand! Bring sandals for her feet!

This my daughter was dead and is alive again.

She was lost and is found!

Requiescat

Although I was accepted to other New England schools (I'm a smart cookie), I have chosen to go to this college. They say blood is thicker than water for a reason. My sister's husband is a professor of biology here. Honey and Nick are really my best friends. My plan is to major in English and Education and become a high school English teacher. I am nuts about plays and poetry. The mysteries they reveal about human nature never cease to thrill me. I am absolutely in love with Shakespeare. Poor Nick, as a scientist, the secrets of all things human are denied him.

It is orientation this week, but I haven't even left the house. I am Honey's confidante, have been since I was old enough to listen. Honey is full now of a story about faculty happenings that I find disturbing but, I confess, intriguing. She tells me that, at a party about two weeks ago, Nick went to bed with the wife of a history faculty member. Or he tried to, anyway (he had been drinking like crazy). Apparently, it was Nick who told Honey about how this woman had tried to seduce him. (Honey was lying on the bathroom floor with her brandy bottle at the time!) Nick confessed to my sister after the party simply because he felt guilty. He had never been unfaithful to her before. When she heard the news, Honey went into shock. Her fit (she gets these—she's like a china doll) lasted almost a week. Apparently, Nick was downright happy with the condition of Honey's pardon. As long as they never went over to George and Martha's again, she decided, she would forgive him.

Honey told me about her hysterical pregnancy—the one that led to Nick's marrying her. I was one of the first to know. The only reason her body blew up is because she wanted Nick to act. Which he finally did—the fake pregnancy really had nothing to do with wanting a baby. It had to do with wanting Nick. On the night of the disaster party, she said the older married pair talked about their son—all the stages of his life. As she was listening, she knew that she didn't just want Nick, she also wanted a child. The desire came from a very deep part of her. She was terrified of having one physically, though. She always has been. It's called tokophobia. Profoundly wanting a child didn't change that. And you can tell by how much she's drinking lately, she knows that the fear is not going away.

Honey says the real story of the night, though, was not about raising or having a child or about adultery. It was about how this history professor George announced the boy's death—he said a telegram had just come with the news.

Braying Martha (that's what Honey called her) broke down and cried when she heard him. But it turned out the death wasn't a real death, because the son wasn't a real son.

Although Nick and Honey thought the boy was real at first—the couple talked about him all night long, in detail—it turned out he was completely made up. It shocked Nick when he found out. Honey said she was so drunk she hadn't gotten the part about how George and Martha actually were not able to have children. Nick had to tell her later.

Nick kept singing this snatch of a song "Who's Afraid of Virginia Woolf?" after he and Honey got back from the party. He sang it like "Who's Afraid of the Big Bad Wolf?" He didn't know what the tune meant but he figured it must be connected with the imaginary child. As they were leaving, he had heard George singing it again, meaningfully as it were, to Martha who was weeping at her imaginary son's death. "Isn't 'A Big Bad Wolf' children's language?" he had asked.

Nick didn't seem to want to probe any deeper than that. Honey also was content just to let it go. Looks to me like neither of them really cared what the song meant.

I, on the other hand, am fascinated. I think the wolf symbolizes Martha's meaningless life, or maybe her and George's meaningless lives without a child. The idea of pointlessness—represented by "no child"—terrified them as though it were a wild animal. They were probably better off when they entertained the illusion that they had a son—for protection against "the wolf"—although it's possible too that they will be more human now without the made-up child.

After the unsettling party and its aftermath, Nick went back to his laboratory in peace and Honey continued to fear what she now knew she most wanted: having a child. Honey easily adopted the bottle as a pacifier in what has become her own childless gloom.

Rise and Walk

I was not your mother. I was your playmate. I'm not sure I know what a mother is. I leave you in better hands than mine, I do know that—dear Bob, dear Ivar, dear Emmy.

When children become corrupt, it is their mothers who cause the corruption. That's what your father, Torvald, said to me. Is it true? Is anything he told me true? Is it corrupt to abandon one's children? I don't believe that forging my dying father's signature out of love for him and for my sick husband was wicked. I also don't believe it makes me a liar, even as Torvald said. Will my leaving you darlings make you sad, then angry, then wicked? If I surrender you to the governess to raise you completely, will that make you corrupt?

I don't think so, but I don't know. There is a lot I do not know.

I think you are better off in Anne-Marie's care than in mine. No one names her a squirrel or a lark or a sparrow and calls it love. What kind of an example would I be to you? Anne-Marie will look on you as she did on me when she raised me: in a kindly way but as a source of income for herself, all the same. She won't attempt to be the model of a married mother, but she will meet your basic needs.

Anne-Marie said she has contact with her daughter since she gave her up for the job of raising me. They write to one another now. Maybe once I am grown, I can make contact with you darlings again. Maybe then I will be able to explain everything. Maybe.

Though he used to call me with words of saccharine affection, just now Torvald called me a hypocrite, a liar; he said I have no values, no sense of duty. He just discovered I borrowed money—8,400 kronor—for a trip to the warm South away from this cold country to save him when he was dying. Did I know my extreme love for Torvald would lead me to forgery? Did forgery cancel out my act of love? In the eyes of the law, as Torvald himself insists?

I don't know. There is a lot I do not know.

Those three crystal moments—when I gave birth to you three children—those were the happiest moments of my life. Will I ever recapture them? In anything I do, in any place I go, in any new relationship I make?

I learned recently about a slave-mother in America who killed her own daughter so the girl would not experience slavery, in all its brutality, as she herself had done. I read about it in one of the hundreds of documents I secretly copied to repay the loan I forged—though I only learned recently that signing my dying father's signature for him was a crime. I didn't know. There is a lot I do not know.

Norwegian slavery isn't brutal, unlike American. It is not one race treating another like property. It is not the domination of black over white—rather it is men treating women as if they owned them. Our kind of slavery is even worse than American, I think, because it has all the trappings of affection—it is more like clonedom than slavery. I was my father's clone as a child and so his ideas became my ideas, and then I married Torvald and his taste became my taste. I did tricks for my husband so I could please him. As I had been father's doll-child, so I became Torvald's. They both robbed me of personhood. They got away with it because it is accepted behavior. I am female and they are male. Torvald, do you understand what a sin you both committed against me?

It is not too late for me to build, to discover the life you and Father never allowed me. In order to do so, I must rise and walk. I must rise and walk out of the doll house.

Like a clone, I have no identity of my own.

Do you hear the door slamming?

I see wild and terrifying territory before me: the valley of darkness.

I will dwell in the valley until the bitter loneliness of experience transforms me from doll into human being.

Royal Silence

The Tower of London? He who will be crowned king? His uncle Gloucester treated Edward and his younger brother, York, like everyday children—not royalty. The hapless young unicorns he threw into Caesar's tower, the slaughterhouse of Clarence, their uncle. Edward, I am told, secretly shared his younger brother's trembling at the place. He appeared strong, though he too was timorous.

Four rose-red lips, four ivory arms, and a book of prayers: into nine dead things two living boys were transformed through blood. Even Tyrrel, suborned by Gloucester, and even Dighton and Forrest, suborned by Tyrrel, knowingly choked on their bloody deeds as they would on a dose of venom, poisoning brain and nerves.

When my two boys, my children, were butchered, God slept. God slept when the hunchback spoke of killing the smooth-skinned lambs. When Gloucester came crying a wolf's tune into the world from his own mother's womb, yes, God slept.

I, Elizabeth, Elizabeth the powerless, sat by while a boar, a toad, not a snake, envied my boys and smote them as Satan smote Adam and Eve through guile. Easy guile, for my boys were only boys. The slaughter of innocents.

Where is God's justice now? Is their Grandmother Margaret right? My little ones but victims of God's scourge? God's scourge of the house of York for all its wrongs? A divine scourge through Gloucester, who is finally king, as he so long desired—Richard III? Was Richard III's mother, Margaret, right about God's justice through murder of young angels?

Or rather, are they not, as we, sacrifices to the divine silence?

Strawberries, Overripe and Soft

The mother is coming into the dining room, the mother whose family I almost saved by telling the truth—I left her and her children vulnerable to the disease. By remaining silent.

I dream that his family and everyone else on this polluted island are slain by the cholera. If they are, I will be alone with the exquisite one.

The other night when I could have rid myself of the attraction by speaking to the boy, I chose not to. Though I am German and he is Polish, I still could have communicated with him as normal human beings do. I could have spoken a few ordinary words on a mundane subject in French, a language we both know. The quotidian exchange would have returned me to reality. It would have shattered my artistic imagination, source of corruption.

But why not nurse the intoxication?

There is nothing more pleasant or more intense or more alive than being transfused with love for a beauty that is godlike, as I have been since I arrived in Venice.

Aschenbach and Tadzio.

Should I write our names like a lonely and unrequited lover in the sand?

Already on the comfortable gondola I rode in on my way here, I felt myself letting go.

Now I don't seem to be able to control what I successfully repressed through the severest discipline, the most stringent routine. At the time not long ago when, at the mercy of a strange travel lust, I left Munich for Venice. I was a successful novelist, known and respected throughout Germany.

I was like Saint Sebastian, suffering for my art; unlike the saint, of course, I did not suffer for God. Or is my art my god? Has it become my god? This love now for absolute beauty in the form of a fourteen-year-old boy-child?

Now being an artist is more like being the devil than the martyr.

Lately the older women who look after Tadzio have begun to call him away when I approach. Their calls pierce me like arrows—the humiliation those cries and whispers make me feel remind me of the insight I have when I wake from those horrible, wonderful dreams of orgy, of lust unshackled: I do wrong.

What is happening to me? Why this letting go?

I was married once, though my wife died young and my daughter married early. I never had a son.

I have written all my life about the importance of upright living. Excerpts of my fiction have even been printed in children's textbooks: my characters model heroism, sacrifice, restraint.

But we artists follow two gods. Dionysus, the god of letting go, though hidden in my heart for many years, has emerged. Since this recent wanderlust, he has done battle with Apollo for supremacy over my soul. Dionysus appears enraged that he was impotent for so long. However, I can pretend that I still pay homage to the familiar god, the god of restraint—can't I?

I don't talk to the object of my desire—communication would break the spell.

I only gaze. And young Tadzio is mesmerized by my fascination.

I may be able to possess the darling without forcing myself upon him, without giving into a moment of frenzy—two methods I am prepared to take but only if I must.

My heart has blackened but it is also perfectly pure: my feeling of love contains lust, lust that is prepared to express itself at any cost, but my love is also the fervent worship of the human and the ugly for the beautiful and the divine.

There he is again—near the sea—on the beach with his friends. He seems to rise out of the water like an eagle ready to fly toward the sun.

I was right to kneel, to put my head against the door of his room in our hotel.

In the silence of the night, I bowed my head in worship: my royal one, my angel, my god.

The sun glows above us, the sea extends beyond: Tadzio's voice rings with the music of words unknown.

I am surrounded by the beauties of the world.

My face is moist.

Dye?

Dripping?

The barber's work—the barber who encourages fifty-year-olds in love.

I, in my degenerating body, wanting to be physically worthy of youth...

...what is happening to me?

...why this weakening? This physical feeling of letting go?

...the spoiled strawberries

I ate them a few days ago...

Overripe and soft...

Take This Gift

I understand how a young person can attract an adult. In a sexual way. I took a seventeen-year-old boy to bed for a night when I was twenty-seven. I met him on the bus. He was a high school student, and I was a teacher. I must have felt that night something of what you felt when you first took my clothed, full breasts into your hands—I was eleven and you were my uncle. You had an age. I know now it was thirty-eight. But then you were: my uncle.

I was a child, and you were a child in a kingdom by the sea.

Is that how I should talk to you? As though you were a child again? If we had been children together—children by the sea—then we could both have given the sea monster our glimmering young bodies. We could have fed ourselves to him together.

Real monsters only prey on the young, you know. Only on children. Only the shininess of youth attracts a real predator. Were we both eleven, you and I? Mine is the only case I know for sure. I can only guess that someone preyed on you, too. When you were a child.

Youth is a beautiful thing, isn't it? It calls out to the adult for spoiling. That weakness, that innocence is difficult to resist. To be the first to give an intimate touch, to do all the steering, to have the power. I learned something of that attraction, the attraction of predator to prey, on my one-night stand. That was ten years after I left you. For good.

Men can't leave them alone—breasts. If they don't unwrap them, they touch them, if they don't unwrap or touch, then they ogle them. But only if the orbs are celestial, only if they are young. Older aging breasts do not satisfy, do they Uncle Peck? Not in quite the same way.

That first photo shoot when I was thirteen—that was all about breasts, wasn't it? I was terrified of that magazine, *Playboy*. I have since learned that *Playboy* is where women split their body from their soul. Women who are naive or vain or who want or need money. There may be other reasons, too. But I made the split when I was quite young without an erotic periodical. The split most women are able to resist until death. Necessity seizes them then. I was one of the naive. *Playboy* wouldn't consider a picture of me until I turned fifteen. That was what you told me. We were just practicing, you and I. You told me you had loved me since I was a baby. And I believed you. You assured me, so I opened my blouse for you at the photoshoot. You see, I was just a child, only a child in the kingdom by the sea.

Some people say I am grateful to you, Uncle Peck, that now you are dead I enjoy going with your spirit on long drives. Some people say I am grateful to you for a gift, for giving me the gift of survival. You know what? I would rather not have been given that gift. I would rather not have had to learn that particular skill. I still envy people who have never had to. I envy them in the way a homeless girl envies another girl her warm home.

I sensed right away that you were a nice man: you often did the dishes for your wife, you worked long hours without complaining, you helped the neighbors shovel the snow, mow the lawn, fix the car. You were sweet and kind and mellow but strong. You were good with children—especially teenagers and preteens. All these things made you likeable. They made me like you.

But you became obsessed with me—your young niece. Or did you become obsessed with my body? You didn't want Aunt Mary's body, I know that, or her happiness, though she was your wife. You never forced yourself on me, it's true. You pretended I was making all the decisions though I was a child and you an adult in a child's kingdom by the sea.

Remember that scholarship I won to study Shakespeare in college? You once said I had a fire in my head, and you had a fire in your heart. What happened to the fire in my head once I entered college? I became an alcoholic and flunked out by the end of my freshman year. And I have since realized: it was not your heart that was on fire—though you gave it as your reason for drink. It was your loins. My body—my breasts—set them aflame. You called that flame love and it confused me. Now I don't know what love is.

I was physically and emotionally attached to you by my eighteenth birthday.

That birthday we spent in a hotel room. That was the afternoon I left you for good. I realized my "love" for you and your "love" for me was sick and I needed to leave you forever.

I was eleven when you began our sexual relationship. Seven years: I was ages eleven through seventeen. On my eighteenth birthday I knew I was old enough to end it. Ages eleven through seventeen still belong to the kingdom: the kingdom by the sea.

Uncle, you took as many years to die of drink after I left you as it took you to ruin me. You had two sick addictions—one to your child-niece and one to the bottle. Was the one much worse than the other, do you think?

I know you had a hard time in the war, though you rarely talked about it. It must have been horrific; but did you have to wrap your misery up and put a bow on it and convince me it was a gift? Did you have to say to me for seven years something to this day I still do not understand: Take This Gift?

Acknowledgments

In addition to Katherine's own unique talent for evoking the powerful images embodied in this collection, the publication of Gasping for Air would not have become a reality had it not been for the painstaking review of the manuscript by editor Michael Fleming of Brattleboro, Vermont, the guidance and support of Katherine's Mount Saint Mary's colleagues Marcos McPeek Villatoro and Johnny Payne, the assistance of her sister Anne Marie Candido, and the essential efforts and moral support of her daughters Emily Crafton and Heidi Logan. I wish that my wife Katherine was here to see the publication of her work.

Don Brueck
December 2023

Katherine Brueck earned a Ph.D. in Comparative Literature (English, French, Russian) from the University of Illinois. She taught for over 35 years at Mount Saint Mary's University in Los Angeles, where she served as Professor and English Department Chair. Dr. Brueck contributed scholarly articles to journals in a variety of humanistic disciplines. She authored *The Redemption of Tragedy, The Literary Vision of Simone Weil,* State University of New York Press, Albany, 1995. In this work she developed a theory of Christian tragedy based upon Simone Weil's mystical Christian Platonism. She spoke on Simon Weil at colleges and universities throughout the United States and England.

A talented poet, Katherine published a poetry collection *Voiceless Love,* Finishing Line Press, 2016. She contributed sonnets to a variety of literary journals, including *Blue Unicorn, The Lyric,* and *Troubadour.* She gave poetry readings in Tri-City Michigan with the Rustbelt Roethke Creative Writers Group and locally in Southern California.

This present collection of poetic stories was Katherine's last creative work before her passing in October 2020. In addition to her own unique talent for evoking powerful images embodied in this collection, the publication of *Gasping for Air* would not have become a reality had it not been for the painstaking review of the manuscript by editor Michael Fleming of Brattleboro, Vermont, the guidance and support of Katherine's Mount Saint Mary's colleagues Marcos McPeek Villatoro and Johnny Payne, the assistance of her sister Anne Marie Candido, the moral support of her daughters Emily Crafton and Heidi Logan, and the dedicated oversight of its posthumous publication by her husband Don Brueck.